D0698987

DOING THE VOICES

DOING THE VOICES

Jeremy Brooks

1986

Viking Salamander

First published in 1986 by
The Salamander Press, 18 Anley Road, London W14 0BY, England
in association with
Penguin Books Ltd, Harmondsworth, Middlesex, England
Viking Penguin Inc., 40 West 23rd Street, New York, New York 10010, U.S.A.
Penguin Books Australia Ltd, Ringwood, Victoria, Australia
Penguin Books Canada Ltd, 2801 John Street, Markham, Ontario, Canada L3R 1B4
Penguin Books (N.Z.) Ltd, 182–190 Wairau Road, Auckland 10, New Zealand

British Library
Cataloguing in Publication Data
Brooks, Jeremy
Doing the voices.
I. Title
823'.914[F]   PR6052.R582/
ISBN 0–948681–01–2

Set in Linotron Baskerville
by Hewer Text Composition Services, Edinburgh.
Printed and bound in Great Britain
by Hazell Watson & Viney Ltd, Aylesbury, Bucks.

For Janice and Robert Stone

All the birds that ever were
Both real and imaginary are gathered here
Under this huge homely tent of blue
Invisible to anyone but you

ACKNOWLEDGMENTS

'I'll Fight You' first appeared in *Winter's Tales 4*, Macmillan, 1958. 'A Value' first appeared in *The New Review* Volume 2 Number 13, April 1975.

CONTENTS

I'll Fight You

'The object of this operation,' said Epsom, 'is torches.' He glared down at us a little defiantly, and then once more marched off down the beach, turned abruptly on his heel, and marched back to where we lay, an irregular, indolent line of bodies sun-drugged on the baking stones.

'*Torches*.'

'Torches,' said the Crow helpfully.

'If possible, *large* torches. Most important of all is one of those big lantern torches, the sort that stands up on a table and has a battery that lasts for months. I admit that makes the operation more hazardous, but it is better to—to—' Epsom searched the flawless sky for a phrase, and found one: 'better to aim at the summit and achieve the foot-hills than to aim at the foot-hills and never rise above the plain.' Aware that he had permitted himself an extravagance, he frowned severely and continued hurriedly with his exposition.

'Method,' he said. 'Diversion by Wrongful Arrest.'

Into the field of my unfocused gaze there now swam Kathy, materialising, it seemed, out of the flat, shimmering sands between the shingle and the sea. She was walking diagonally across the sands towards us, but as yet seemed unaware of us; carrying her head forward a little to examine the sand immediately in front of her toes, which she pointed deliberately as she brought them down, as if in the preliminary flexings for a dance. At her heels bounced and rolled her ridiculous little dog, Wiggy, who had been so often an instrument of our tentative friendship. Kathy's arms were folded behind her back in one of those strained contortions of the painfully shy; her light summer dress moved as she moved, in a near dance across her knees.

'Smith!'

'Sir?'

'You're not listening, Smith. Dreaming again. Women, I shouldn't wonder. Now then, what is the object of the exercise?'

'Torches,' I said. '*Large* torches.'

'And the method?'

'Diversion.' It was always Diversion, there was really no satisfactory alternative on a large-scale operation.

'What category of diversion?'

'Basic Scrimmage?' I hazarded. It was my favourite—a chance to pay off old scores on the excuse of realism. An artificial snort of laughter from Gregory told me that I had guessed wrong. I threw a pebble at him and gazed with apparent indifference towards the sea. Kathy was nearer now, walking more slowly, no longer pointing her toes. I realised that she had seen us but, glancing round, saw that none of the others had spotted her. Dewi was lying on his back, his thin arms folded behind his head, his eyes closed.

'A fine sergeant you are!' snorted Epsom. 'Be losing a stripe if you don't watch it, man! Wrongful Arrest is the method, and don't you forget it, Smith. You start any of your unnecessary scrimmages and you'll be for it. Dewi, you're a furtive-looking element, will you take on the diversion for us?'

This was kind. Still enfeebled from recent polio, Dewi could not run fast, was often a liability on occasions like this; but it would never have occurred to us to exclude him, for that reason, from our activities. It was typical of Epsom that he should find a way of solving two problems with a single kindness. Dewi was grinning abstractedly, already planning his moves.

'Smith, if he can stay awake, will be Observer. And don't fire,' Epsom added softly, ' 'til you see the whites of their eyes.' I knew what he meant. Excessive nervousness had often led me to give false alarms.

'We'll leave the big lantern to you, Red, no one else could do it. You may not be able to manage it, at that, don't take any chances. Don't forget you're on their black list, they'll be watching you. If you can't coincide with Dewi's diversion, leave it. Crow, as many U2 batteries as you can manage. Gregory, I want one—just one—of the long type, takes four or five U2s, with the big adjustable spotlight. You'll be directly opposite Red, so time yourself by him. Peredur, second line diversion. Get right in at the back and keep your eyes on Smith. If he gives the signal, make a dash for it, with as much noise as you can. If they catch you, say you saw someone passing in the street and wanted to catch them. Okay? I think that's all. Peter, here, will be in the background as usual as witness for the defence if there's any trouble. Don't anyone expect any help from me, I've got my own problems. Any questions?'

'Where do we reassemble, sir, and when?' Gregory, a stickler for form, invariably had a question and loved to phrase it, as he thought, correctly. His blank, unnaturally smooth face, glistening with sweat, flushed now with delight at his own cleverness.

'As usual,' said Epsom shortly. It was a stupid question. After every one of the hocking expeditions so far carried out by Epsom's Resistance Group we had made our way independently to the premises of the Music Club, and there sorted and apportioned our loot. Gregory, as Quartermaster, kept his books there, and would have been the first to protest if we had decided to regroup elsewhere. But that was Gregory: 'a man,' as Epsom had once defined him, 'impelled by some awful genius to draw attention to his own stupidity.'

Peter Hatchett was consulting his watch. 'Zero minus twenty-two,' he offered in his emotionless, scientific voice. 'It's ten minutes' walk, there's no hurry.'

'Last cigarettes, gentlemen,' announced Epsom, bringing

out a stub from the breast pocket of his shirt and feeling for matches. 'Hey, Smith, where the hell you think you're off to?'

'Istanbul,' I said rudely. Kathy had passed us, not twenty yards from where I was sitting, without a glance. I had walked a few yards away from the group when Epsom called; and, turning now, I saw Dewi sit up, catch sight of Kathy, and stiffen, his eyes fixed on my face. Epsom too had looked past me to where Kathy was crouching by a shallow pool of water, and then he glanced once at Dewi and back to me. We stood staring at each other, while Gregory peered hopefully from one to the other, longing for the clash of wills, which, he estimated, would send me flying for comfort to his arms, but which, in fact, never quite materialised. Epsom pinched out his upper lip between finger and thumb, drawing it down, in an habitual gesture, over his protruding front teeth; then let it go so that, as he suddenly grinned, it flew up like a blind and the teeth popped crookedly out.

'Ten minutes,' he said, grinning. 'And, Smith, remember— Careless Talk Costs Lives.'

'Take a jump, Jones,' I said; and lounged easily away, kicking in front of me the rusted tin can that earlier had been the target for our lazy throwing. I could feel the back of my neck smarting from the sun.

I called her name softly as I approached. Her back was towards me, where she crouched by the pool and it was too easy to startle her. Now she turned slowly.

'Hello, Bernard,' she said, without a single inflexion of surprise, smiling up through her hair. At once she turned back to the pool, reluctant as always to let me read her face. 'This little fish,' she said, 'he was stranded. I've put him back in the middle but he just won't make an effort. If only he'd swim around for a bit I'm sure he'd feel better. Silly little fish!'

I crouched beside her at the edge of the pool, over-conscious of my audience up on the shingle. I could see nothing in the pool. Kathy pointed, her forefinger, like mine, indelibly stained with black school ink. 'Look, there!' 'Where?' 'There, silly, just under my finger. Now I'm touching his tail.' A little puff of sand exploded in front of her fingertip and I had a glimpse of some minute creature darting away across the pool to bury itself once more in the sand. 'Oh good!' cried Kathy, 'he's all right now. Did you see?'

I said I'd seen. I thought it was probably a bullhead, capable of living between tides in a hollow of damp sand, but I didn't tell Kathy: she thought she had performed a timely mission of rescue.

'Let's walk,' I said. 'I've only got ten minutes.'

'Oh, why? Oh, Bernard, you've *always* only got ten minutes!' Kathy gulped a little with horror and turned her head away, appalled, as I was, by this naked admission.

'I've got something on with the boys. I promised I'd only be ten minutes. I'm sorry.' Kathy said nothing. After her last remark any sort of silence was impossible, so I floundered on. 'You haven't been to the Music Club lately. Someone said you were ill. And you weren't on that Eglwysbach hike—that was fun. Dewi fell in the lake.'

'I know,' said Kathy. Mentioning Dewi was a mistake. Nobody could have failed to remark the diligence of his attentions to her in recent months, nor to conclude that they were favoured by my own neglect.

'I don't expect you missed me,' said Kathy, laughing slightly to show how little it mattered one way or the other. 'I expect you had a good time with Isobel, didn't you?'

'*Isobel?*' I laughed contemptuously at the idea, shaking my head at the folly of idle gossip.

'She can be great fun, can Isobel,' said Kathy reprovingly. 'Someone told me you and she had *tremendous* fun on the Eglwysbach hike.'

'That Dewi! I'll wring his rotten little neck!'

'It *wasn't* Dewi!' cried Kathy triumphantly; and she started dancing away from me across the sands, with Wiggy barking

15

insanely at her plumping heels. I had to run to catch her and
instinctively put out my hand, clutching her arm, to stop her
dance. At once Kathy stopped, as if my touch had turned her
suddenly to stone. She stood as rigid as a statue, her brown eyes
wide; and I stood facing her, still holding her arm, panting
slightly. Our immobility after the sudden violent movement
now lent any movement, any words, an awful weight of
meaning. I dropped my hand. Kathy turned her head away.

'Kathy. Listen, Kathy. I just walked with Isobel, that's all. I
had to walk with somebody. You know what those hikes are.'

'I know.' The 'hikes', as we all by now accepted, were little
more than organised necking parties; which was why, having
no one to neck with, Dewi had fallen into the lake.

'Anyway,' I said, 'I did wish you were there, so there.' Kathy
said nothing; and then, for no reason, started laughing, running
in circles round her yapping dog, her skirt swirling wide out,
flaring, twisting into a tight spiral, untwisting, swinging like a
bell. I grinned uneasily. Kathy could do this; pluck laughter
out of the air and gather it suddenly about her like a rich robe.
It was a quality peculiar to her, almost a form of power.

'Anyway,' said Kathy, as she came to rest once more at my
side, 'I couldn't have come, 'cause I've been ill, so I'm *glad* you
enjoyed yourself with Isobel!'

'Now look, Kathy . . .'

'Oh, do look at Wiggy, Bernard, look!'

Wiggy, pretending he was a gun-dog, was stalking a herring
gull: nose down, bottom up, tail twitching. We watched in
silence, leaning slightly towards each other so that our
shoulders just touched, an overtly accidental contact. I felt
Kathy shiver, as if she were cold, and I thought automatically:
someone walking over her grave. The herring gull, tiring at last
of the ridiculous animal approaching it, heaved itself into the
air and drifted casually away. We went on standing there,
saying nothing, neither of us wishing to lose that tiny treasured
area of contact through which, as if we had no part in it, some
vital exchange was now proceeding.

'Smith!' Epsom was shouting across the sands. 'Smith ahoy!' I jumped away from Kathy, turning at once to wave my acknowledgment.

'I shall have to go, Kathy.'

'What is it? What are you all up to? Can't I come?'

'Not possible. I can't explain, but it just wouldn't do. Will you be at the Music Club tonight? It's a dancing session, you know.'

'I know what you're going to do, Bernard,' said Kathy, looking at her feet.

'You don't, you know.'

'I do.'

'Don't be silly.'

'I do know, and I'm not silly, it's you who's silly. I know more about you than you do, Bernard. I know—oh, *everything* about you! And I think it's silly, so there!'

I became very angry. 'You don't know what you're talking about, Kathy,' I said roughly. 'You stick to things you understand, like—like that damned dog of yours.'

Kathy looked helplessly towards her adored dog, and I saw with horror that her eyes had filled with tears. Epsom was calling again, I had to go. I wanted to say something, even to put out my hand to touch her smooth brown arm, but it could not be done. I started walking away, turning after a few paces to say, in what I hoped was a gentle voice, 'See you tonight, then?'

'I don't know,' said Kathy, not looking at me, her voice so low I hardly caught the words. I began to run, cursing under my breath. The group were already on their feet, scrunching lethargically up the shingle to the promenade. When I arrived among them Dewi would not look at me. Gregory was grinning lugubriously, and if I had not avoided him would surely have produced the sort of fatuous remark that would have forced me to hit him. 'Zero minus nine,' murmured Peter Hatchett reprovingly. I took my place beside Epsom as we walked up towards the town, glancing back once to where Kathy still

17

stood, a small figure out on the sands, her hand held out for the
dog to jump at.

'How was she, mate?' asked Epsom.

'All right. Been ill, it seems.'

Epsom raised his black eyebrows at me. 'Oh, Smith, Smith,'
he mourned, 'you must be the last person in this town to
discover that! Man in heaven, you don't deserve a dead whore!'

'Go stuff yourself,' I said.

Long observation had taught us that there was a period, on
Friday afternoons between four-thirty and five, when Woolworth's was more crowded with shoppers than at any other
time of the week. A crowd, although it made my job as
Observer more difficult, was an essential condition for the
success of a hocking operation. Red Glyn Jones, of course, had
been known to pull off a one-man sortie when the shop was nearly
empty; but even his panache and recklessness would quail
before the task Epsom had today set him, without a crowd and the
knowledge of a well-trained commando group supporting him.

The big lantern-torch, which it was Red's job to secure, was
needed for our 'bothy'—a deserted shepherd's cot—up on the
slopes of Tal-y-fan, overlooking the coast road. Here were
stored now most of the arms, ammunition, food and cooking
equipment which we had patiently assembled throughout the
summer term. Circumstances occasionally forced us, when
carrying new items of equipment up the mountain to this
stronghold, to spend the night there, so the lantern was really
essential, for it was much too far to carry any large quantity of
paraffin. The smaller torches, and the batteries, would be
stored in the little hut up in the woods on the shoulder of
Nant-y-Gamar, not far from the town. This was illuminated by
an Aladdin lamp whenever we had cause to use it after dark.
The Nant-y-Gamar bothy, first home of the Resistance Group
and once well-equipped with weapons of offence, had now been
denuded in favour of Fynnon Gyrach, mainly for strategic

reasons. As Epsom had pointed out, one of our first duties when the Germans invaded would be to blow up the bridges and seize control of the mountain passes. For this purpose our arms dump on Nant-y-Gamar would be useless, for it was on the wrong side of the River Conway and not within reasonable striking distance, cross-country, of the A5. It was an unanswerable argument and it had to be, for the labour of transporting our slowly garnered stores ten miles across the mountains had been immense. Left to ourselves, without Epsom's ruthless leadership, we would never have completed the operation. As it was, much of the summer holidays had been used up on this carry and we were all, I think, feeling a little bored with the whole thing. It had come immediately after some of us had just finished sitting the School Certificate examinations: a time when a man most needed his freedom. Girls had been neglected, games, hikes and parties missed, while the carry was on. Now, we felt, we really deserved a rest. We had made our contribution to the defence of North Wales. Our major stronghold was fully stocked, the cadre of the Group well-knit, trained and confident of its military value. Once today's operation had been successfully carried out, we would be able to sit back and enjoy the rest of the summer holidays, waiting with easy consciences for the invasion to begin.

There would be all the time in the world to put things right with Kathy . . . if that was what I wanted.

From the end of the soap counter nearest the central doors I watched the Group take up their dispositions as planned. It was vital that I should keep in visual touch with the main actors, for my job was to co-ordinate evasive action if anything should go wrong. As usual, I could feel the hollow of nervousness inside my chest, and I kept glancing at the clock, wishing that the action would begin and quickly be over.

But Dewi had to be given time to arouse suspicion against himself. Seven minutes were allowed for this; he and I had already been in the shop for five minutes before the rest of the Group started making their individual, unobtrusive entrances. I saw Red come in, hands in pockets, whistling softly through his teeth. He walked straight past me without a blink. At the far end of the shop Peredur suddenly appeared and stood gazing hopelessly at an array of aluminium saucepans. I saw him glance once at the clock, and then towards me. I scratched my left ear: 'All's well.'

Dewi's field of activity was the counter of tools that ran parallel to the one of electrical equipment, where most of the hocking would take place. The Crow's U2 batteries were further down the same counter and he would lack the full protection of Dewi's diversion; but it was never difficult to fill one's pockets with small batteries when the crowds were there. I had some anxious moments before I could find a position from which I could see Dewi and at the same time be seen by Peredur, and twice was obliged to stand on the platform of the weighing machine in order to see over the heads of the shoppers. Dewi, picking up and putting down articles from the counter in front of him, doing up and then undoing his jacket, glancing to left and right and back over his shoulder, was the very picture of nervous guilt. Despite our part-time enmity, where Kathy was concerned, I had to admire him. One glance would tell any wide-awake adult that he was about to pocket, or had already pocketed, some unpaid-for article.

I could see neither Epsom nor Peter Hatchett, but I was not worried about them. Gregory, hovering among the crowd near the long flashlights, was waiting for Dewi's diversion to get under way, but Red, typically direct in his approach to any problem, had already got himself jammed up against the counter and was handling, with an expression of concentrated insanity, the heavy lantern that was his target. I watched him switch the thing on and flash it at the ceiling; then he put it back on the counter, plunged his hands into his pockets, and stood frowning bleakly at the thing as if plunged into the depths of fiscal calculation.

Suddenly things started to happen around Dewi. With

impeccable stage-management he had succeeded in arousing the suspicions of the attendant not of his own counter but of the one opposite, where the torches were. The girl had left her post at the till and was now standing over Dewi, hands on hips, and calling to her opposite number at the tool counter, from which, she supposed, Dewi had been stealing. Dewi cringed away from her as if afraid that she would strike him down.

At the far end of the shop Peredur was standing on tiptoe to catch my eye. I scratched my right ear—'Diversion under way'—and moved forward to observe the proceedings more closely. As I did so Red passed me, sauntering unhurriedly towards the door, the lantern hanging undisguised from his hand. I saw at once that Gregory was going to muff his chance; having been too far away from the counter when the diversion began, he could not now dart forward, grab his torch, and make off without pause. I had been in his position too often to feel anything but sympathy for his plight.

An older woman in a blue overall had now joined the two girls talking to Dewi, who had shrunk into himself like a sea-anemone, his head between his shoulders, his fists bunched in the pockets of his sports coat, his eyes darting from side to side, from face to face, as if looking for a route of escape. He was playing it out, I thought, to the last drop, refusing to turn out his pockets, playing dumb. A portion of the crowd, realising that something was going on, was beginning to coagulate around Dewi and his interlocutors, forming, as it were, a crowd within a crowd, and it was into the outskirts of this that I now began to insinuate myself. Across the heads of the contestants, only a few yards away but separated from me by a wall of bodies, I could see Peter Hatchett gloomily observing the scene; and behind him, with a box under his arm, a vacantly interested spectator, Epsom.

Suddenly I felt my arm clutched and, turning, found Kathy beside me. 'Bernard!' she gasped, eyes wide, face white, '*do* something, it's Dewi, they think he's stolen something, you must *do* something, Bernard!'

Grabbing her shoulders I tried to turn her away, whispering urgently: 'Leave it, Kathy, leave it, it's nothing to do with you, just leave it, will you?'

But she would not be deflected. Twisting out of my grasp, her eyes blazing, she gasped: 'Well, if you won't do anything, I *will*! You're—you're a *coward*, Bernard!' And she plunged away into the crowd. Horrified, my mind whirling with possibilities, I followed.

Dewi was now being led away. The Supervisor—if such she was—held his arm just above the elbow, her face set grimly, while Dewi hung away from her, cowering, muttering his denials in a voice near to a sob. Behind him marched the girl from the electrical counter, closely followed by Peter Hatchett, ready as always to confuse the issue with his well-wrought pomposities.

Kathy exploded in front of this procession like an avenging angel. 'Let him go!' she cried, 'he hasn't done anything, I was there all the time, I was with him, he didn't take anything, honestly he didn't, just because he's got a limp you think . . .' The crowd closed once more around them and for a moment I could neither hear nor see what was going on.

When I had wriggled through to the front of the crowd I saw at once that Kathy had made an absolutely appalling blunder. Her intervention in itself was not disastrous: since Dewi was quite innocent, despite his refusal to empty his pockets, Kathy could do no more than increase for him what was already an embarrassing enough role. But now—now, I saw, she had turned aside, looking for further witnesses of his innocence, and had found Epsom. Seizing him by the arm, she dragged him in front of the furious Supervisor. 'This boy was there,' I heard. 'He'll tell you Dewi didn't take anything, he was standing right beside him, I saw them both, he'll tell you . . .' Kathy, almost sobbing her words, was near to hysteria.

'Well, bring him into the office then, I'm not going to argue with you children here. Now come along all of you.' The Supervisor, pushing Epsom and Kathy ahead of her in her fury, dragging Dewi, forged on towards the back of the shop.

Epsom looked round desperately. Whatever it was he had in that box under his arm, I knew that he hadn't paid for it.

Peredur, peering anxiously towards all this commotion from his post by the aluminium saucepans, once more caught my eye. Almost without thinking I brought my hand up and laid it flat as a plate across the top of my head: 'Emergency Scrimmage.' Instantly there was a terrible clatter of pots and pans as Peredur swept them on to the floor, and then he was darting and diving towards us down the crowded aisle between the counters, straight into the face of the little caravan of which Epsom and Kathy formed the unwilling head. As he came Peter Hatchett made a lunge towards him, and for a moment they were both sprawled back against a counter of lampshades; then Peredur broke away again, with Peter after him, straight into Epsom's arms. I dived towards them, grabbed Kathy, turned her, and pushed, so that she went tottering away out of range of the wild fight that was going on almost at the Supervisor's feet, and which I now joined.

Several people were shouting, and a man grabbed my shoulder and pulled me away from what he thought to be some sudden adolescent flare-up. I twisted out of his hand, and seeing Epsom in full flight on the heels of Peredur I too turned and ran, leaving Peter Hatchett to apologise, as he later told us, to the Supervisor for having 'failed to stop the boy who knocked the saucepans down.'

Peredur, Epsom and I reassembled, panting and grinning, in the Gentleman's lavatory beside the Town Hall. 'You're a good team, boys,' said Epsom, 'I thought I was for it that time. That Kathy of yours, man-diawl!' He looked at me suspiciously, but I shook my head. 'Never breathed a word,' I said. 'She must have followed us.'

'That girl,' said Epsom, 'she'd follow you into hell's mouth for a kind word, Smith.' He began to undo his cardboard box. 'What do you think of this?'

Nestling neatly in the box, lovingly packed in corrugated paper, were a paraffin cooking stove, a detachable saucepan stand, and a complete nest of aluminium cooking pots with folding wire handles.

'Smokeless,' said Epsom, 'that's the point. It's all very well, doing our cooking over a fire at the moment, but we couldn't risk that once we become operational.'

'Good show, man,' said Peredur, who had already adopted the slang of the service in which, two years hence, he would be casually killed.

'That thing uses paraffin though, doesn't it?' I asked. Epsom sucked his teeth and nodded. 'Yes, it'll mean another carry, I'm afraid. Not very arduous though. A few gallons would last for months, and we can easily hump up a couple of gallons each.'

Peredur looked across at me and grimaced. 'That's not going to be popular, boy,' I said. Epsom began packing up his box, saying nothing, and I wished I hadn't spoken. I knew that he looked to me for support in his battle against the waning of the Group's enthusiasm. As we left the lavatory I turned, without thinking, to the left, heading back the way we had come. Epsom and Peredur turned right, and stopped. 'Hey!' yelled Epsom, 'where are you off to now, Smith?'

'Woolworth's. See if Dewi's okay.'

'You're not, you know.'

'I am, you know.'

'You're bloody not, son. That woman won't be forgetting your face in a hurry. Just let her see you and Dewi together and she'll tumble. We're going up the Room. Come on.'

'See you later,' I said. I began to move away, fully expecting an explosion of violence from behind me. But nothing happened. Puzzled, I glanced back. Epsom was still standing where I had left him, sucking in his lower lip, apparently undecided, with Peredur waiting impatiently a few paces further on. Then Epsom called again, more quietly, 'Hey, Smith!' I stopped again, and he began walking quite slowly towards me. He waited until he was right on top of me before saying, in a mild voice, 'It's that Kathy, I suppose, is biting you, eh? Well, for Pete's sake be careful, boy, will you? Don't go mucking the whole shoot up now.' He looked at me solemnly for a moment, plucking at his upper lip, as if there were much to be said that ought not to need saying; and then he grinned, his great yellow teeth gleaming in the afternoon sun, and punched my shoulder rather harder than was necessary. 'Go on then, hop it, and remember—the Agag walk!'

'The Agag walk'—one of Epsom's favourite obscurities; he would not have used it to me if he were angry. Once again an impending clash had been, as they always would be, averted. There was always a point in our disagreements, and this was what Gregory could not appreciate, when one of us realised that the other was immovable, and, without fuss, withdrew. No issue could be worth the tragedy of that final rift.

In fact I was lucky: it didn't prove necessary to go anywhere near Woolworth's to reassure myself of Dewi's release and Kathy's well-being. As soon as I was back in the main street I saw them, walking side by side towards me, Kathy pushing her bicycle along the edge of the pavement, the dog still at her heels, and Dewi, looking tired, limping more than usual, slouching along beside her with his hands in his pockets, his eyes on the pavement in front of him: a subdued pair. For a few moments I hung about on the opposite side of the road, putting off, as always, the embarrassment of the first greeting. Then Kathy saw me, waved, and made as if to cross the road. I waved her back and crossed towards them. Dewi grinned uneasily and then suddenly turned away.

'Kathy, I'm sorry . . .'

'Oh, Bernard, I'm sorry . . .'

We both spoke at the same moment; both waited for the other to go on; and then spoke simultaneously again. Kathy started to laugh. 'I hope I didn't hurt you?' I said.

'Serve me right if you had. Oh dear . . . Have you forgiven me, Bernard?'

'You couldn't have known. If you hadn't dragged Epsom in you might even have been a help . . .'

'I didn't mean that. I mean—what I said.'

'What did you say?'

'Don't you remember?'

'No,' I lied.

Kathy peered sideways at me and started laughing again. 'You do!' she said. 'You're a fibber, you're an old fibber, Bernard!'

I blushed. Dewi said abruptly: 'Well, what did you say, Kathy?'

'It doesn't matter,' I said, 'it was nothing. Come on, we've got to get up to the Room. Let me push your bike, Kathy.'

'I called him a coward,' said Kathy, 'and he's not.'

'No, he's not that,' said Dewi shortly.

I wheeled Kathy's bicycle, and she walked beside me, with Dewi on her left. At Lloyd Street we turned towards the sea, then right, along the promenade, walking slowly because of Dewi: a small, sandy boy with painfully thin limbs and a tough mind. The sun was less hot now, but the surface of the promenade, baked by the long heat-wave, threw up its stored warmth like a hot-plate after the power had been switched off. The soles of my feet were uncomfortably hot, my socks sticky and unpleasant.

'Did it go all right in there?' I said.

'Yeah.'

'Did they make you turn out your pockets?'

'Yeah, I turned 'em out. Properly foxed, the old dame was.' He snorted, imitating, as we all occasionally did, Epsom's sardonic laugh. Kathy laughed softly, too. Dewi asked if the operation had gone according to plan.

'I think so. I'm pretty certain Gregory boobed, though.' I was not sure how much Kathy knew; the existence of the Resistance Group was supposed to be a secret from the rest of the Music Club members.

'Gregory would,' said Dewi. 'A damp character, that one.'

We were talking across Kathy, without looking at each other, and I could feel, as Kathy must have felt, the tension between us like a tangible object, a vibrating wire of the unsaid and the unsayable.

'Will you be in tonight?' I asked Kathy again, thinking that this time, in front of Dewi, she was more likely to give a straight answer.

'I might,' said Kathy, as before. Holding her head down, she glanced up and sideways, an achingly familiar gesture quite innocent of coyness, and I knew that she was teasing me, knew that she would be there. And I suddenly became afraid again: afraid that at the last moment I would find some excuse for not being there myself; afraid of what I felt about Kathy; afraid of the complete involvement that would follow, as it had before, if—as I surely would—I danced with her all evening and then walked home beside her through the amorous summer night; and afraid, too, in an obscure way, of Dewi, of the violence of his emotions, and of the twisted sympathy I felt for him.

'One of these days,' said Dewi, hobbling stiffly along on his spidery legs, 'I'm going to learn to dance.'

The premises of the Music Club, known to us usually as 'The Room', were in the attics of an hotel owned by the Crow's father and now in use as offices by the evacuated Inland Revenue. Mr Raven, 'the Vulture', occupied a small annexe at the rear of the building, and the Room was far enough away from this for us to be able to make, in the evenings, as much noise as we liked. Windowless, the low eaves stacked with furniture, the Room was the very centre of our lives, an island of adolescent logic amid the dangerous lunacies of the adult world.

Dewi and I watched Kathy swoop away on her bicycle like a bright bird, with Wiggy running and yapping beside her; then we turned in to the hotel entrance and climbed the stairs in silence. The rest of the Group were already assembled when we emerged through the trap-door into the Room; an altercation was going on between Epsom and the Crow. The afternoon's loot—Red's big lantern, half a dozen U2 batteries, a smaller torch, Epsom's cooking stove—was laid out on the floor. Gregory, crouched beside it, was entering each item meticulously in his Establishment Book.

'What's up with you two?' I asked Epsom. He was clearly very angry, standing with his legs astride, hands on hips, his black eyebrows drawn down in a scowl. The Crow, hands pocketed, was leaning with apparent nonchalance against one of the main timbers of the roof, his head bent, a smile of contempt on his lips. Epsom turned furiously to me.

'When I plan an operation I make it as foolproof as I know how, but it's only foolproof as long as everyone does what he's been told to do, no less and no more. This silly bastard thinks he's clever because he got away with a few bars of chocolate. Chocolate! I ask you!'

'Very useful stuff, chocolate,' I ventured.

'Highly nutritious,' agreed Peter Hatchett, wagging his long head solemnly.

'That isn't the point, Smith, and you know it. Chocolate wasn't planned for, we weren't covering that counter at all. He could easily have been caught, it could have upset the whole bang shooting match.'

'But I wasn't caught,' said the Crow mildly. The Room virtually belonged to him, but he knew better than to use this, as he might easily have done, as a weapon of immediate defence.

'You weren't, but, by God, I almost wish you had been. That would at least have made you see sense. It may seem a small thing to you, Crow, but imagine what would happen if we were operational and you started messing around with little ploys of your own like that. You'd be risking lives then, and I won't have it!'

'Operational!' the Crow sneered. He had never acceded to Epsom's conviction—or deliberate assumption—that an invasion was imminent. Epsom turned away in disgust, his colour mounting. 'Get that stuff hidden away, Greg, as soon as you can. You can check out the stove, and the cooking pots, and the lantern, to Fynnon Gyrach. The rest goes to the bothy.'

'Do you want me to enter the chocolate?' asked Gregory.

'Damn, no! Make the bloody man eat it, and I hope he chokes on it. Chocolate, my God. Apart from anything else, it's dishonest.'

'*Dishonest?*' said the Crow, gaping.

'Yes!' snapped Epsom, turning on him with sudden violence. 'Stealing, if you fancy a nice blunt word, Raven. Petty thieving! Sounds nice, don't it?'

'And what the bloody duck you think you've been at, boy?' spluttered the Crow. There was a pause as Epsom walked over to the trap-door; everyone was looking at him, even Gregory.

'Requisitioning of essential war materials,' said Epsom coolly. 'Come on, Smith.'

I heard a titter of laughter as we went down through the hatch but knew that he had won his point. There would be no more 'petty thieving'—not, at any rate, on any of Epsom's expeditions.

When we came out on to the promenade we found that Dewi was limping breathlessly along beside us.

'I want a word with you, Smith,' he said.

I looked at him in surprise and was suddenly filled with terror. He stared straight in front of him, his face set, beads of sweat clinging to the soft fair hairs on his upper lip. I thought: No, no, I don't want anything to do with this. Epsom said, as if he had not heard Dewi's words: 'I want a fag, man-diawl,' and we turned aside to one of the glass-sided shelters at the edge of the promenade.

'If you two would rather,' said Epsom delicately, with a stub of cigarette between his lips and an unlighted match poised above its box, 'I'll beetle off for a bit?'

'You stay where you are,' said Dewi, not glancing at him. We leaned against the wooden posts, one each end of the shelter, facing each other, with Epsom standing between and a little way off, like, I couldn't help thinking, an umpire.

'What's biting you, lad?' I asked casually, making great play with the lighting of my Woodbine.

'Were you thinking,' Dewi asked, 'of turning up for the dancing session tonight?'

'I was thinking of it.'

'Well, I shouldn't, if I were you.'

I saw Epsom's eyebrows go up. He must have been as aware as I was what all this was about, but such direct, open attacks as this were not within our convention. Where girls were concerned rivalries had to be conducted as if they were not taking place at all.

'Well, you're not me, so you don't have to worry.'

'Get this clear, Smith,' said Dewi in a flat voice, 'Kathy's my girl, you keep your dirty hands off her.'

'Hey, hey!' said Epsom, 'that's fighting talk, Dewi.'

'I'll fight him.'

'Don't be stupid,' I said.

'I'll fight you,' Dewi said again. He would have, too. I could see his frail little body was strung up for action, the knuckles white knobs on his thin brown hands.

'That's crazy,' I said. 'Fighting never solved anything yet.'

'You're scared, Smith.'

This was so ludicrous that it ought to have been funny, but we didn't laugh. Looking at him there, poised like a cat, no one could have been sure that he would not succeed in throttling me to death before my hands ever closed on his wasted body.

'Smith isn't scared of anybody, Dewi,' said Epsom severely, 'and you know it, so don't talk rubbish.' This was partly true; I would fight anybody with my fists—it was words I was scared of. 'If you've got something to beef about,' Epsom went on, 'let's hear it, and stop arsing around.'

Dewi was trembling so much that he could hardly speak. It must have taken an immense effort of will to have got as far as he had done. 'He's got to leave her alone!' he suddenly cried. 'I won't have him mucking her about. I've seen him at it before, he plays her along for a bit and then he drops her flat, it's just a game for him, that's all, just a bloody game to pass the time between one fanny and the next. Well, it isn't a game for her, and it isn't for me, and I'm warning him now if he doesn't leave her alone I'm going to kill him.'

The silence that followed this was terrible. I drew a deep breath, as if I had something to say, but I hadn't.

'Let's have less talk about killing and fighting,' said Epsom, 'it upsets me, I've got a weak heart.'

'I'll fight him,' said Dewi. He seemed to have got these words stuck in his mind, and I guessed that he had rehearsed the scene over and over to himself before screwing up his nerves to force it upon me.

'So what happens then?' asked Epsom. 'Either he wins or you win and what does that prove? Only that he's stronger than you, or you're cleverer than him. It doesn't make one right and the other wrong, and it doesn't,' he added offhandedly, 'seem to give Kathy much of a say in the matter.'

'You leave Kathy out of this!' muttered Dewi.

'I should have thought,' I said mildly, as if the whole discussion were academic, concerning strangers, 'that it was all a matter for Kathy to decide.'

'Kathy can't cope with sly bastards like you, Smith. She just wouldn't understand your sort of nasty mind. You've fiddled with practically every woman in the town, but Kathy's the last person in the world to realise that. You're not fit to walk the same street with her, and you've got to leave her alone.'

This sort of talk was incredible, impossible, I couldn't argue on these terms. Even Epsom, I saw, had withdrawn himself, I assumed for the same reason that now made me say: 'You'd better jag it in, Dewi, I'm not going to argue with you. I'd have to become a hermit if I wanted to avoid seeing Kathy, and I don't, and I won't, so you can take it or leave it. Now bugger off, man, I've had enough.'

Dewi also had had enough, he was sagging like a dead lily. 'I've warned you, Smith,' he said weakly, too exhausted now to pretend there was anything in the world he could do, short of murdering me in my sleep, that could lend substance to his threats, 'don't say I didn't warn you.'

When he had gone Epsom and I sat smoking in silence for some time, staring out to sea where a fishing-boat hung motionless in the haze. 'Poor old Dewi,' said Epsom absently after a while. Then, later: 'You'll have to make up your mind, boy, one day. Which frightens you most—getting the girl or losing her?'

'I don't know,' I said, simply and truthfully. It was to such isolated rocks of truth as this that my friendship with Epsom was anchored.

'There's nothing,' Epsom said, 'you can do about Dewi. He's making his own hell. Kathy was your girl before Dewi was ever out of hospital.'

This also was true. I may have dallied, from time to time, with others; but anyone in the Music Club would have acknowledged, without hesitation, that Kathy was my girl: though they may have wondered, considering the worth of my prize, what madness made me treat her like dirt just when our intimacy seemed most firmly established.

I had sensed that Epsom's mind was not now really concentrated on my problem. Something quite different had caught his attention, something on which, I knew from experience, he would brood for weeks, perhaps months, before coming to me to share his thoughts. Thus it had been before the inception of the Resistance Group: I had known for weeks beforehand that his own inactivity in the face of what seemed, at that time, like certain and immediate invasion, was intolerably galling to him.

We left the shelter and walked on down the promenade towards the point at which we would separate and head for our respective homes, and tea. 'What's up, mate?' I asked, as our steps slowed down. 'That business with the Crow?'

'The Crow? Oh, that. No, no, he'll be all right. It's just this fighting business—ah, hell, I don't know.'

'Fighting business?'

'What I said to Dewi. Where the hell does it get you, eh? If you're on the right side—if there ever *is* a right side—and you win, you just make it more certain than ever that you'll have to fight the same enemy again, some day. You know why we're fighting this war? Because we beat Germany in 1918. And if you lose, what's the odds? It just means the right idea will have to come to the surface some other way. It always does, you know, haven't you noticed that? Whatever some moral pioneer thought a hundred years ago, we take for granted today. Or am I wrong? Did some of them have to fight and die for their ideas way back in the beginning? Or *not* fight, and die? Hell, I dunno. I'll have to think.'

'You sound as if you've gone loony to me.'

'Perhaps I have, Smith, boy. You know me—muddle, muddle, toil and trouble, but the spell works out in the end. Well, I'm off. See you in the Room tonight?'

'I don't know.'

'Oh?' Epsom raised his eyebrows, and then again gave me his sudden toothy grin. 'Your problem, son,' he said. 'I wish you joy of it.'

He turned off jauntily down Vaughan Street, and I watched him go without alarm, too full of my own crisis to allow any weight to his; not knowing on this, as it turned out, last day of Epsom's Resistance Group and the first—as I still think of it—of my love for Kathy, that he was starting down that thorny lane which was to lead him, before any of us were yet dead, into the lonely cell of a pacifist's gaol.

A Value

Macphee placed the bomb in the very centre of the round iron table and laid his newspaper carefully alongside it. The chairs around the table appeared to be empty, but Macphee's eyesight was now so bad that he could not be certain some child or dwarf was not crouching in one of them, so he walked round behind each chair, an arm trailing in the sitting space, before going up to the bar to get his pint of bitter. No dwarves.

Macphee was not afraid that anyone might recognise the bomb for what it was: at a casual glance it appeared to be an old, much-handled, leather-bound book, the lack of any lettering on its spine suggesting perhaps a Victorian autograph album. But it would have been dangerous to leave the bomb on the table if anyone had been near enough to tinker with it. The thing, though perfectly safe to handle if one knew what one was doing, was not fully primed and needed to be treated with respect. Years of research, of delicate adjustment and subtle creative thought would be wasted if the thing went off prematurely and in the wrong place.

For the purpose of buying beer, particularly the first pint of the day, Macphee liked to have both hands free. He'd had some trouble with his hands recently. Getting a pint of beer up to his lips without a proportion of it spilling down the front of his overcoat required two hands: the texture of his coat lapels attested to the many minor accidents that had preceded this discovery. Macphee wasn't sure whether his shaking hands were the result of his diet, which for two decades now had consisted largely of beer, or of a growing nervousness, which he was quite aware of in himself, as the day for action approached. He would have preferred to believe the latter, but suspected the former. He knew that he was not afraid: what he felt when he thought about his bomb was not fear, but awe. His nervousness was the perfectly natural reaction of one who had never before in the fifty-six years of his life found himself required to take even marginally violent or positive action; and it was not even the consequences of action that made him nervous, only the possibility of failure through ineptitude.

He faced the fact, as he ordered his pint, that he drank too much beer. But then, too much for what? Soon, very soon now, there would be no beer, for him or anyone else. Or—and his mind made the sideways leap it always did when caught making an absolute assumption—the whole process of producing and consuming beer would be so different as to require a whole new mental approach, to which present attitudes would be irrelevant. He dismissed the subject, comfortably.

'Gaudeamus,' said Macphee, before he took the first deep draught of bitter. The barmaid grinned at him, although she knew he couldn't see her grin; through his thick pebble spectacles her face would be a featureless pink blob. Poor old Macphee always said that before the first drink of the day. She didn't know what the word meant—something religious, she thought—but she liked the way he always said it.

'How's the bomb coming along?' she asked.

Macphee laid one finger against the side of his nose.

'I thought you said you could keep a secret?'

'I can. There's no one in here but us two, dear. I only unlocked two minutes ago. Hello though, here's Mrs Scuttle coming for her jug of bitter, you'd better go and guard your . . .'

'Ssssh!'

Macphee carried his second pint back to the table, cursing himself for that far-off indiscretion. He didn't believe the girl dangerous; she thought of him, he knew, as a harmless loony who made incomprehensible jokes, but it bothered him that his 'joke', which was no joke to him, was the one she chose to keep reviving. Perhaps he should stop using the pub? But he found it difficult, these days, to modify his physical habits. He had taken his breakfast here for so many years now that a change would confuse him, interfere with his concentration.

Macphee took a good mouthful of beer and then, remembering, allowed half of it to dribble back into the tankard. He would have to make his pint last the half-hour or so it would take him to decipher, with his magnifying glass, the main points of the news. Two pints was a meagre meal, but he now had only a few pennies left in his pocket. Later in the day he would have to walk through to Covent Garden and get some cash off his agent. It was a task he always put off to the last possible moment, for it took him out of Soho, along streets where the smells and sounds told him little, where the texture of pavements, the distances between doorways, were not familiar enough to guide him without conscious thought. He hated having to think about anything but the bomb.

If poverty is equated with need, then Macphee was not poor, for his needs were minimal and his income, though small and getting smaller, perfectly sufficient to them. In fact Macphee considered himself rich, since an absurd chance had decreed that not since his late twenties had he been obliged to do any work that was not of his choice. Even the school teaching which had preceded his good fortune had been quite enjoyable; it had been amusing to cultivate his image, among the boys, as a mad poet, a benign figure of fun whose classes were good, at the very least, for a laugh. The three or four boys he encountered who enjoyed his sombre wit on its own terms, who read and understood his poetry, had become lifelong friends. The only thing that enraged him was the low quality of the Latin and Greek primers which the curriculum imposed upon him; though comparatively recent publications, they were only marginally better than those which he had disliked so much during his own early schooldays. Without giving the matter much thought, Macphee sat down and devised the first of a series of primers and textbooks which within a few years became, and remained, standard teaching manuals throughout the country. As soon as his income from royalties achieved a steady £600 a year, Macphee left the school and never again, until the necessity of devising and delivering his bomb became apparent, worked at anything but his poetry. Three generations of classical scholars know what a 'macphee' is: it is either a book, or it is a rendering of a classical tag more accurate in the spirit than the letter: Argumentum ad verecundiam—Because I say so.

Macphee recognised the social injustice inherent in his freedom. It was an absurdity that a man could live for a quarter of a century on the fruits of a few months' amusing labour. But, Macphee reasoned, there was at least a certain poetic justice in it, for without this modest stipend he would never have had the unattached intellect which had made it possible for him to conceive of the need for the bomb, nor the time to devote to all the research that had gone into its construction.

A nice quart of apple fritter. Mrs Scuttle's daily phrase, just heard again for something like the three thousandth consecutive time, chased itself around Macphee's mind. It worried him that the word 'fritter' was in the singular. You can't have a quart of a singular solid. A quart of prawns, winkles . . . A quart of sand—sand counted as a liquid. A quart of pebbles . . . A quart of quartz? Aha! Nice, but no: a quart of quartz chips. On the other hand, 'a quart of apple fritters' would not rhyme with 'bitter'. *Bitters* were something else, an aromatic additive. You could have a quart of bitters, but that wasn't what Mrs Scuttle wanted. At least she was being consistent if not grammatical.

Such musings on the vagaries of living language were the ever-present slurry that lubricated the surface of Macphee's mind, a light counterpoint to the more weighty thunder of dead languages that swelled in the depths below.

Without looking at his hands, Macphee rolled a very thin

cigarette, using a black liquorice paper. He didn't particularly like liquorice paper, but had found himself increasingly prone to light white cigarettes in the middle, with occasionally dangerous results. It was easier to aim the match flame at the tip of a little black stick than at the tip of a little white one. Macphee was not a wholly unwordly man and was well aware to what extent these consistent physical details—the thin black cigarettes, the candy-striped stick, the ritual exclamations in Latin and Greek—contributed to making him, in the square mile of streets from which he seldom strayed, a 'character': a benign, because wholly predictable, element. Therein lay his safety. He knew people said, 'Here comes poor old Macphee.' He had often heard them say it, for his hearing had become phenomenally acute as his eyesight deteriorated. It made him smile. They meant that he was slightly dotty, nearly blind, obviously impecunious, usually alone. But in any of these streets, were he to stumble, mistake a turning, meet an unexpected obstacle, or be attacked by strangers, a dozen helping hands would move to aid him; all, probably, less safe in this world than he. Poor? Above the thin tortoise neck, behind the magnified watery blue eyes, Macphee carried his store-house of riches with a safety and sureness none of those who came to his aid would ever know.

But no more than they was he or anyone else in the world safe from those busily burrowing moles, out there in the big world beyond Soho, who were blindly undermining, with their self-obsessed tunnels, the palace of civilisation which man had built from nothing and which would return to nothing once it fell. Macphee turned to his newspaper for the daily evidence.

He was selective in his reading. He had to be. His reading-glass, though powerful, could frame at a size visible to his painfully focused eyes only three or four words at a time. To decipher a whole column was a slow business. Of most of the world's events the headlines, if he could understand them—for they had an increasing tendency to whimsy—would tell him all that he needed to know; in most cases, more than he wanted to know. An airliner crashed here; drought and famine there; a department store on fire; a king deposed and exiled; a city destroyed by earthquake; a child killed by its parents; a cure for cancer postulated; a man landed on the moon . . . all natural events: reading the details would illuminate nothing. Macphee was in search of material relating to the manufacture and delivery of his bomb. It was not that he needed any strengthening of his resolve: once he had seen the necessity for action there had never been a moment of doubt. But it was interesting, in a purely academic way, to see how a few items in each day's crop of news, when laid side by side, screamed aloud a message which, it seemed, nobody but himself could hear.

Another ex-Cabinet minister, he read, a man renowned for the depth of his moral fervour and the probity of his private life, had fled the country under an assumed name to join his boyfriend in Chile, stopping only in Lichtenstein to pick up the off-shore money he had stashed away over the years of building up his bubble-businesses, now collapsing behind him like a line of dominoes. Marginal, Macphee thought. It was happening all the time, and was only a symptom of the disease, not the disease itself. Interesting, in that he had predicted this particular form of breakdown long before it had become, in the inaccurate phrase journalists used nowadays, 'epidemic'; but significant only as an effect, not a cause. The fact that certain politicians and businessmen were now being hustled by events into revealing the absolute extent of their abandonment of ethics was simply a mark of their superior understanding: they knew how far their molish tunnels had gone, and, unlike others, appreciated how much they had weakened the fabric of the palace they were plundering. It was time to go; let the thing collapse about others' ears. Anyway, it was perfectly natural that if a man should be willing to disadvantage himself, spiritually, by seeking both power and wealth, he should use those tools to compensate himself for his profound losses. It had ever been so. It was only recently, though, that a breed of men had emerged who had, and sought, nothing else but power and wealth, and did not even know that there was anything else to seek. Perversely, Macphee felt compassion for this type of mole.

TEACHERS REJECT PAY AWARD Macphee read quite easily, the first word more or less postulating the other three. He didn't blame them, but wondered if this wasn't just another strategic move in their long struggle to establish a living standard comparable to that of a manual labourer? He doubted if it was a sign that it had at last occurred to them that they were the most important people in the world, and even if it had, probably only a small proportion of the profession was truly qualified to make that claim. Had it ever appeared likely, or even possible, that those responsible for settling the level of teachers' salaries might say, 'All right, we admit your claim, and are prepared to award you a higher basic salary than that common among accountants, dentists and Members of Parliament, providing only that in order to qualify for it you will submit yourself to a Value and Literacy test devised by our colleague Hamish Macphee . . .' then Macphee's bomb might never have been necessary.

But this, it was clear, was never going to happen. Only a politician could make it happen, and politicians were themselves blinded by the same fallacy of Immediate Measurable Results as the poor teachers.

This, of course, was the plughole down which value was escaping—to be replaced by price. If children could now be taught only to estimate the economic advantage of knowing something—which had already been happening when Macphee was a teacher—and not to appreciate the value, for its own sake, of the knowledge, then one might as well wind up civilisation like a failed business: hand it over to some molish Official Receiver to collect what debts were owed to it (from Macphee, for instance; but how would he pay?), pay off its creditors (Macphee among them; but the account would never balance), and announce the incorporation of a new firm. Because if anything was certain it was that if the people who were destined to take the day to day decisions that governed the life of the country continued to put price before value they would take the wrong decisions, and the old firm would collapse. And yet, how could they not, if they had never been brought face to face with a real value in their lives?

The country's budget of £80,000,000,000 for 'defence', Macphee read, was to be marginally cut, but a further £900,000,000, not part of that budget, had been allocated to the development of a new kind of fighter plane . . . The Arts Council announced that it could not be responsible for the National Theatre's current deficit, but would raise its annual grant by £20,000 next year; an N.T. spokesman described the theatre's position as 'ludicrous' . . . This was too obvious and frequently noted a juxtaposition to stimulate Macphee; and anyway there was something simplistic about assuming that contemporary art, the natural enemy of politicians, should expect generous treatment from them: the hanged man does not pay his executioner. Macphee was concerned with the roots, not the fruits, of his ailing tree.

An area of Africa five times the size of the United Kingdom had gained its independence after four centuries of colonial rule. Fighting had broken out in the capital . . . A nuclear device had been exploded in Antarctica, despite protests . . . Nothing, nothing. The longest-surviving heart-transplant patient had died. Nothing. The Prime Minister, speaking in her own constituency, had said . . . nothing.

PARLIAMENT TO DEBATE RAISING
SCHOOL LEAVING AGE TO 17

Macphee swallowed, lowered his reading-glass, closed his eyes for a moment to rest them, then scanned along the headline again. This was not really necessary. He knew he had not mistaken the import of the words, either in their abstract or their personal sense. As to the latter, the chill of a fine sweat on his forehead told him all he needed to know. Certainly this news was only of symbolic importance, but then, it was symbols he dealt in, it was only through symbols that the most deeply buried force-lines of cause and effect could be understood.

Had the bomb been ready when the school leaving age was raised to sixteen, Macphee would have delivered it then.

Oh blindness and folly! The precious ichor thinned, and thinned again.

Macphee folded his newspaper carefully and stowed it, together with his reading-glass, matches, and tobacco, in one of the deep side pockets of his overcoat. He scooped the bomb carefully towards himself across the table top and stood up, clutching it to his stomach with both hands. He felt for once reluctant to guide it into its safe inner pocket, would have liked to have walked through the streets with the bomb held high and triumphant above his head, but knew that this could not be done. He was not mad. Besides, there was his stick to be found.

He searched the back of his chair, then of neighbouring chairs. It was a distinctive stick, painted in red and white spirals like a barber's pole, and a necessary extension of his eyes. For a moment he panicked.

'Betty!' he cried, vaguely towards the bar, 'My stick! I've lost my stick!'

'Don't panic, duck. It's here. You hung it on the bar.' Betty sounded warm and reassuring, but to another customer she added in a low, slightly sour voice, 'Daft ha'porth. Every morning he does that. Poor old sod, he's half gone.'

Macphee heard, but gave no sign of hearing. Betty had a right to speak of him as she felt, and anyway he agreed with her that such repetitive behaviour was ridiculous. But there was little point in trying to change faulty habits now; it was too late; and anyway, he might never visit this pub again. He gave Betty an engaging, self-deprecating smile as he collected his stick, and heard her say, when she thought him out of hearing, 'He's all right, really. There's them as can see as is worse.' Macphee liked that, rolled the words around his head as he fumbled through the door. There's them as can see as is worse. Lovely.

He came out into D'Arblay Avenue and turned right, towards the junction with Berwick Street. Offices here, railings, a flight of steps, more railings, then he could edge in towards a wall. Some fat trout in corduroy trousers—*swish*-swish, *swish*-swish—squeezed between him and the wall. Silly cow, couldn't she see he was . . . ? No. Macphee modified the thought as he picked up the demented mutter of dramatised complaint that was spilling from her lips. No blame.

On the corner of Berwick Street he heard his name called, and a moment later a girl took his arm. One of the girls—which? He sniffed, stumbled around in his senses for a moment, then got it right. 'Elvira! Hello! How nice!'

'Been having your breakfast have you?' asked Elvira. A curious acidity, as of permanent fear, came through the very powerful scent she was wearing. He could dimly remember what she looked like, which meant that he must have known her for about ten years—not so much of a girl these days. How long could they keep at it?—to forty? Fifty? It was one of the many things he would never know now.

Elvira clung tightly to his arm all the way down Berwick Street to the market. Macphee told her about losing his stick, and what Betty had said. 'Do you think I'm "half gone", Elvira?' he asked, really wanting to know.

'Course not!' Elvira cried indignantly. 'You're lovely. My Dad always said, absence of mind is presence of mind elsewhere.'

'Did he, now? *Did* he? What an extremely perceptive remark. I must remember that.'

Elvira left him at the corner of Broadwick Street. 'Got a spot at the Forty-One. Strip and jiggle. It's nothing in the mornings. You all right?'

'Fine, fine!' said Macphee, although he could feel tension mounting in him like a confined spring. 'I know just where I am, where I'm going. So glad I met you, Elvira.'

One of the girls. There were so many of them, those girls, and they changed, came and went, so often that it was difficult for Macphee to distinguish between them without some individual sign, such as the acidity of Elvira's body odour. But in their numbers lay much of his own security: successive landlords of the warren in which he lived had difficulty enough in assessing the commercial status of known trade without bothering themselves about the worthless few square yards of attic space occupied by Macphee. He had been given notice to quit often enough, but had always ignored it with a calm heart, and somehow the threat always went away. Macphee would have been astonished to learn of the efforts—sometimes verging on strike action—made from time to time by the girls to keep their talisman.

From the point at which Berwick Market narrows to the alley that leads into Brewer Street, Macphee could travel home by smell. He could have taken a shorter route, but this was safer, and richer: coffee shop, delicatessen, café, garage, another delicatessen, an off-licence, a trendy clothes shop with pop music murmuring . . . the dangerous crossing of Wardour Street, then all the familiar sensations of Old Compton Street, a warm, teeming reality which he knew he might be experiencing for the last time. This was the world the moles were blindly undermining, which they could standardise out of existence without having the faintest idea of what they were doing.

Macphee stopped outside the paper shop which sold newspapers and magazines from all over the world. He got out his reading-glass and, bending his long back and neck towards the racks outside, scanned headlines in languages he only half understood. Whatever they were saying it was all music, beautiful music, people talking to people: amuse me, instruct me, excite me, believe me, understand me, love me . . . the corruscating contradictions of human culture.

> *Ne hadde the appil take ben, the appil taken ben*
> *Ne hadde never our Lady a ben heven queen.*

An odd jump there, Macphee told himself, a very odd jump from the Tower of Babel to Original Sin . . . his mind was racing so fast that he'd missed the bit in between. Never mind, it followed, it followed, if only backwards. Ah, coffee shop, coffee shop! The smells! Would this endure? In a world of Value it should, but in what form, and for whom, and how to

communicate this sensation to the primary producers, were
questions Macphee knew he could not solve alone.

'Hi, Hamish. Nice smells, eh?'

A hand touched his elbow and was gone. Another of the girls.
He couldn't identify her, but smiled warmly towards where the
voice had been; then realised that the voice had been attached
to a pair of uncomfortable shoes, one of them loose around the
heel, which he could still hear faintly receding: Doreen. He *must*
try to remember to explain to Doreen about the importance of
comfortable shoes. Pity he'd been so slow—Doreen could have
helped him with the telephone call he had to make. Never
mind. He'd find someone. He moved on.

Del Monicos. He was known here from the old days when
he'd been on brandy, before the business of the pickled liver,
and they had a telephone; but some dim sense of Security made
him discard this possibility.

Turning north again into Dean Street to complete his
three-sided route home Macphee became aware of a public
telephone box ahead, about twenty paces, just inside the
corner of a covered alley. He slowed his steps, turned round
confusedly, tapped with his stick at the kerb as if lost. There
was a strip joint ahead on the left, ten paces, man with a query
Greek query Turkish accent just inside the door, but he'd insist
on Macphee using the house phone, as on a few occasions
before. Tap back south? He heard a firm step, felt his elbow
grasped in firm fingers.

'Hey, hey, Hamish man, you turnin' like a leel dawg! You
cain't be lawst *hee*, this your back*yard*!'

Napoleon. Macphee could smell him now, sweet and musky,
a touch of resin from the woods he worked.

'Not lost, Nap. Just a slip of the memory, that's all. There's a
phone box round here somewhere and I can't quite . . .'

'Right here, man, Baker's Yard. Jee-*sus*, you know *that*! Hey,
you awl right? You look . . . *scattered*, know-what-ah-mean?'

'I'm all right. Look, Nap, now you're here, could you find a
number for me?'

Coaching Napoleon in the technique of using a telephone directory proved to be a long and irksome business. Napoleon, when the system was explained to him, argued that the Parliamentary Press Gallery of the House of Commons was bound to be listed under P, not, as Macphee suggested, under H. He opened, however, the wrong volume, came across C by accident, and read aloud a whole half column of 'Common' before declaring that there was no 'Commons' in *this* book. In reluctant search, at last, for H, he encountered G, and was with great difficulty dissuaded from investigating Galleries. When it turned out that the Parliamentary Press Gallery was listed as a separate sub-heading under the main House of Commons heading he crowed in triumph, slapping the book.

'There you are, man, like I *told* you—Parliamentary begins with P! Why you make it so *difficult*, know-what-ah-mean?'

Macphee apologised, was effusively grateful, and held the door of the telephone box open. Napoleon left, grinning, shaking his head over Macphee's craziness, more proof, if any were needed, that nobody but Napoleon could handle the technical difficulties of life with any real finesse.

The man Macphee asked to speak to, when the Press Gallery answered, had once been a poet, perhaps still was, but had published nothing but political journalism for twenty years. He was not, as far as Macphee knew, a mole himself but lived among moles, earned his living as a by-product of molish activity, and it was unlikely that some elements of molish self-absorption had not rubbed off on him. Nevertheless Macphee remembered him from the far-off days, when they had appeared together from time to time at poetry readings, with mild affection: a small, mouse-coloured man who wrote unexpectedly passionate erotic verse. Although his name was Alex Maxwell he was always addressed, for reasons unknown, as 'Bill'.

'Bill,' said Macphee easily, as if they had recently parted, 'this is Hamish. Hamish Macphee.'

'Hamish Mac . . . ? Good God! A ghost from the past!'

'Nothing ghostly about me, Bill. I'm . . .'

'Of course not, no, it's me that's gone ghostly. Odd to hear you though, after—what?—eighteen years?'

Macphee was impatient with all this. He had found two more ten pence pieces at the bottom of a pocket, but Maxwell was being irritating, saying things like 'political scribblers don't expect to get calls from famous poets . . .' Self-deprecating, an edge of guilt. Macphee let the man give his hearty, well-that's-life cover-up for half a minute, then interrupted.

'Bill, I'm sorry, I'm going to run out of time. I really called—not knowing how else to find out—to see if you could tell me when the house is going to debate the raising of the school leaving age?'

There was a moment's silence. Macphee waited. Had he transgressed some unknown molish code of conduct with his question? Then he heard a faint murmur of voices in the earpiece and realised that Maxwell was simply asking a colleague for the information.

'Well, as it happens,' Maxwell said, rather tetchily, annoyed perhaps at having been revealed as less than omniscient in his own field, 'it's down for today. But, good God, Hamish, surely you can't be interested in *that*! I assure you, nobody else is. All the arguing's over. Everyone's made what capital they can out of it, and no doubt we'll hear the axes ground all over again for the benefit of the press, but the issue's a dead duck. I can't imagine what . . .'

Macphee suddenly found himself angry, and anger begot an idea.

'As a matter of fact, Bill,' he said slowly, 'I believe this is going to be a very important debate—*very* important—for everyone. More important than any of you realise. And I intend to be there.'

There was silence from Maxwell; his journalist's mind was doing what it could with this, on the face of it, insane declaration.

'You mean,' he asked carefully, 'something unexpected is going to happen? Something you know about?'

'You could say that.'

'Hamish—is this a tip-off?'

'Yes, Bill.'

'First-hand source? Dead cert?'

'Absolutely.'

'But—why me, Hamish? Dammit, we haven't even . . .'

'It's in the interests of my source,' said Macphee, no slouch at picking up tones of voice and jargon, 'to have the debate covered as thoroughly as possible. I thought I might benefit both of you by dropping a hint. Mind you, I haven't *said* anything . . .'

'Of course not, Hamish, not a word. Look, you wouldn't like to lunch with me, would you? The debate's down for five o'clock, but they won't get anywhere with it till around nine if things go the way they look. No, tell you what, better still . . .'

Macphee was happy to hear Maxwell's voice cut off by urgent beeps as the time bought by his coin ran out. He had found out what he wanted to know, and had attracted as an observer to the coming event someone whose past dreams and perceptions might enable him dimly to perceive what was happening; possibly, even, why.

Back in Dean Street, he found a pedestrian to hail a taxi for him. There was no point in economising now. In Covent Garden he asked the unaccountably distrustful taxi driver to wait while he fumbled his way up a dark stairway to the office of his agent. Here he secured, after argument, a cheque for £45 and £8 in cash from the petty cash box. Macphee didn't know why this young man, who had become his agent after the death of Macphee's friend and mentor, the founder of the firm, so hated to part with money which was not his and which had come into his possession through no labour of his own; but he perceived that it was so, and therefore made these occasional transactions as easy as possible. He had not been shown a publisher's account for ten years and suspected, correctly, that the young man owed him more than he could easily afford to pay.

51

Paying off the taxi in Shaftesbury Avenue, Macphee identified and entered a shop selling ready-made men's clothing. He bought an overcoat, suitably dark, though he would have been horrified by its cut if he'd been able to see it, and a white shirt. The shop assistant was helpful and attentive and, while Macphee used his magnifying glass to write a cheque, stole two pound notes from Macphee's open wallet, a loss Macphee was destined never to feel.

Tapping his way north up Dean Street again, Macphee wondered about food. Smells of coffee in Old Compton Street had awakened in him an interest in tastes other than beer. Beer was, in many respects, as he had proved, a very complete nourishment; but there were other foods. He remembered a period of his life, long past, when he had been obsessed by kippers. Kippers, and tomatoes, and fresh French bread—he had eaten nothing else for months on end, terminating the episode only when it had become clear that the tenants of neighbouring rooms would tolerate it no longer. Ah, kippers! That had been good. Days of hedonism, days of brandy. Ah, brandy! The past.

He touched the bomb in its safe inner pocket. He was used to its weight there, but it had seemed to grow heavier recently. This, he sanely knew, was an impossibility, but the sensation was real, and dated from further ago than this morning's reading of the newspaper. This must indicate that his readiness to act had itself become a burden, and he should therefore regard today's debate, and the duty it imposed on him, as a relief rather than a challenge. Having worked this out, he did so regard it; and, having done both, admired his intellectual control.

Food. Why did he keep thinking of food? It was unusual, must mean something. Fruit, yes, he was dwelling on fruit.

> *The nectarine his strong tint imbibes*
> *And apples of ten thousand tribes*
> *And quick peculiar quince.*

Macphee did not fancy a quick peculiar quince, but, brooding on fruit, knew suddenly what he wanted. A pomegranate! Yes!

He had to walk to Charlotte Street for his pomegranate, making the usually difficult crossing of Oxford Street by the simple expedient of holding his candy-striped stick out in front of him and stepping off the kerb into the traffic, which, with squeals and hoots, parted before him like the Red Sea. Exciting but dangerous, he thought, as he tapped up the comparative quiet of Rathbone Place towards his pomegranate. Dangerous and foolish. To waste, now, those years of work in a self invited accident would be folly. He was suffering, he knew, from hubris, and must fight to control it.

His pomegranate, hard-skinned, irregular in its rotundity, vague in smell, was waiting for him in Charlotte Street. It was shaped like an old-fashioned anarchist's bomb. He allowed the carrier bag, in which lay his new clothes, to hang from one elbow, his stick from another, and carried the pomegranate in the palms of both hands, like a bomb, back down Rathbone Place, across Oxford Street—letting a sympathetic hand guide him this time—and along Greek Street to the turning which would bring him home.

Pomegranate, he said to the fruit in his cupped hands, what do you remind me of, apart from a bomb? Young love. Oho, Romeo. 'It was the nightingale and not the lark/That pierced the fearful hollow of thine ear;/Nightly she sings in yon *pomegranate* tree.'

Be a bomb, he said to the pomegranate, not a love-tree. Be a bomb! But it was turning into a love-tree as he walked. Looking deeply into the vague blurred form, he began to bounce off things: lamp-posts, pillarboxes, stalls, parked cars, other pedestrians. He dropped his stick, scrabbled around on hands and knees for it, the pomegranate held securely in the hollow between jaw and shoulder, until some kind but, he felt, faintly supercilious helping hand put the stick back into his fingers. All this erratic conduct was unusual in him. He put it down to two things: the imminence of action, the influence of the pomegranate.

In his mind's eye he saw a sixteen-year-old girl's face, so perfect in form and line, so innocent in expression, as to be indistinguishable, in terms of Value, from his mother's. He beamed at the pomegranate, endowing it with a curve of smiling lip painful to dwell upon, a texture of skin so delicate that light could find no reflective foothold and must pass round the forms and come back to illuminate them from behind.

Colour of hair: brown

Colour of eyes: hazel

Distinguishing marks: absence of self-regard.

He felt his upper arm gripped firmly, he was pulled suddenly sideways, off balance, so that he almost dropped the pomegranate, did drop his stick. The bomb slapped heavily against his leg, and the carrier bag swung awkwardly from his elbow. Before his assailant spoke he knew who it was: chewing gum; pipe smoking; touch of asthma: Sergeant Doyle.

'Mister Macphee! You all right, sir? Here's your stick, there now. Wandering along in the middle of the road, it's not like you, is it?'

'Letter from home,' muttered Macphee, with a flash of genius of which he was instantly ashamed.

'Ah, now,' said Doyle, all understanding, 'that can really throw a man, a letter from home . . .'

Doyle started to prattle on in a sentimental way about what letters from home had meant to him and to fine strong men he'd known who had broken down and wept. Soft sod, Macphee thought. It was, of course, obvious why extreme authoritarianism so often went hand in hand with sloppy sentimentality, but that didn't stop yet another demonstration of the pattern from being irritating. Vague muttering about letters from home would not save a known villain, against whom the sergeant had a grudge, from being beaten up while escaping arrest in the police car on the way to the station, or in some convenient back alley. Macphee had heard it happening often enough. He disapproved of villains, but feared Doyles. They were the tools of moles. Macphee moved on along the pavement, as if lost in dreams of home.

He could smell meat. That would be Benson's. He felt the window and doorway on his left, identified them as belonging to a pornographic bookshop into which he had once stumbled, asking unsuccessfully for a copy of Cavafy's poems. He moved on the length of one shop-front and entered the butcher's shop. It was years since he had been in here, but the butcher, a florid, loud-voiced man who lived on bread and jam, hailed him warmly.

'Still with us, Mister Macphee? Well I never. Thought you'd moved on to better things. What'll it be then? A nice bit of veal you was always fond of. A Dutch escallop? I know your tastes.'

Macphee, who never ate veal, for aesthetic reasons, put his pomegranate down on the chopping-table.

'I wondered,' he said, 'if you'd mind splitting this for me?'

'Well,' said the butcher thoughtfully, a touch surprised, 'well, well, have to wipe off me cleaver for that, wouldn't I?'

Was that a refusal? Macphee wondered. He couldn't see the man's expression, could only guess to what degree humour was supposed to enter into this response. He waited.

'I never chopped a pomegranate before,' said the butcher.

'It doesn't have to be in equal halves,' said Macphee diffidently.

'Oh, but it *will* be,' said the butcher, 'it *will* be, Mister Macphee!'

Swish! Thunk!

Macphee winced. So easy. He heard the two, certainly equal, halves of the pomegranate fall apart and rock gently to rest on either side of the wood-embedded cleaver.

'Want 'em wrapped?' asked the butcher, now certainly mocking him a little. 'Togevver or separate?'

'I'll take them as they are, thank you.'

Macphee felt for and found the two equal halves of the pomegranate, drew them together and reunited them. A little cool blood ran through his fingers. The nightingale and the lark. Virgin mother, virgin mistress. Oho, Romeo.

There was a pub on the corner of Daneham Street. Macphee paused outside, consulting his stomach about beer. He was torn. He had to get the pomegranate home, and scoop out the flesh, now of you, now of you: there was that to be done. He had to think about tactics, dress, timing, response to interference. He had to maintain himself in a fit state for action. It was the last consideration which sent him into the pub.

'What have you got there, Hamish?' said a voice, as Macphee set his two pomegranate halves on a table, apparently unoccupied, just inside the door of the pub. He knew at once that he'd made a mistake. This was his drinking companion, the poet Emrys Pugh, a man now, of all times, to be avoided.

'It's a pomegranate, Emrys. Two equal halves of a single pomegranate.'

'It was the nightingale and not the lark that pierced the fearful hollow of thine ear, nightly she sings in yon pomegranate tree,' said Emrys Pugh to Macphee's utter disgust. 'I'll help you eat it. And buy you a beer.' Emrys Pugh went away. Macphee gathered the two halves of his pomegranate and felt his way quietly out of the pub. Oh no you won't, Emrys, he said to himself, I will not have a lousy Welsh poet eat either of the joint owners of my soul.

He encountered none of the girls on his way up the many flights of stairs, dwindling in size, covering and importance, that led to his attic room. From some of the rooms came murmurs of voices, creakings of bed-springs. These sounds called forth no images in Macphee's mind; he had no experience on which to base an image. Love was another matter; had been invested, once, totally in one love-object, and had then been split equally between two; when both had died at once, to punish him for some unknown transgression, love had been withdrawn from circulation.

Macphee's room was very small; in it, he behaved with deliberate care. The two equal halves of the pomegranate were laid side by side, seeds uppermost, at the edge of the circular table beneath the dormer window. The bomb was placed in the centre of the table; tobacco, matches, newspaper and magnifying glass on top of the small cupboard beside the narrow bed. The new overcoat was shaken out, smoothed, and hung on a wire hanger from a hook on the door. With difficulty the new shirt was unpinned from its supporting cardbord and plastic and laid across the back of an upright chair, but this proved unsatisfactory: every time Macphee crossed the room he had to pick up and as it were waltz around the chair, an action which would ultimately, he felt, result in the soiling of the new shirt; so he transferred the shirt to the foot of the bed. His old beer- and food-stained coat was folded and pushed under the bed, joining there a collection of other cast-off garments which provided a comfortable home for a large family of mice. Macphee had a companionable attitude towards the mice, and fed them, when he remembered, with unsuitable delicacies.

Macphee lived frugally, but was not without his pleasures. A current passion was smoked salmon, a single pale membrane of which survived from his most recent purchase. He had, too, an ancient crust of wholemeal bread. Together these provided a delicate counterpoint to the spoonfuls of juicy seeds he scooped from, now you, now you, careful to do equal justice to both, and to leave in both an equal quantity of translucent seeds, for remembrance. It was a good meal. He turned the pomegranate halves face down on the table, took up his magnifying glass, and scrutinised the flesh-coloured domes for signs and portents. He found one. The half which he associated, for no reason but chance, with his mother, was flawless; the half which he associated with his sixteen-year-old virgin lover had a brown, corrugated blemish near the neck. Macphee nodded. He had been right. Flawed. All flawed.

But the bomb, now, the bomb, *that* was flawless! He took it in his hands, weighed it, revelled in the thought of it. A perfectly constructed object—perhaps the only perfectly constructed object the world had ever known, would ever know! He had made this thing, not out of pride, not for self-glory, not to advance a cause or bully others into submission, but simply as a *proof*, the one and only incontrovertible proof of the simplest but most commonly ignored concept: that the Value of an object, artefact or event is not in its result but *as* a result. Put more simply—but, no, Macphee refused to put it more simply. The thing was obvious. The past *is* the future.

He allowed himself to turn over the outer covers of the bomb and let his eye—or rather, his mind's eye, for he was not using his reading-glass—run over the inscriptions.

Adam lay ibbowndyn, bowndyn in a bond/Fowre thousand wynter thowt he not to long:/And all was for an appil, an appil that he tok,/As clerkis fyndin wretyn in here book./It does not slay; nor is it slain./I am that I am./What rough beast, its hour come round at last/Slouches towards Bethlehem to be born?/I am indifferent to all born things, there is none whom I hate, none whom I love; but they that worship me with devotion shall dwell in me, and I in them . . .

Macphee didn't need to read the words, he knew them all by heart. These juxtapositions, random on the face of it, stirred in him a music that could boil blood. He shuddered, shook himself, shuddered again, aware of passing through a point at which it was impossible to distinguish pain from pleasure. He turned a few pages of the outer covers, knowing it was self-indulgence but wanting for once to indulge himself. It would be all pain for the moles, but for him—well, had he not just eaten his mother's head?

Go! put off holiness, and put on intellect/Saying, Peace, peace; when there is no peace./Dust shalt thou eat all the days of thy life./And after the fire, a still, small voice./My father moved through depths of height./In time the savage bull sustains the yoke, In time all haggard hawks will stoop to lure, In time small wedges cleave the hardest oak, In time the flint is pierced with softest shower./Water wears out the stone, not by force, but by falling often./Grieve not over that which is unavoidable./An evil and adulterous generation seeketh after a sign./Tomorrow for the young, the poets exploding like bombs . . .

Macphee breathed deeply, like one handling a heavy object. He ought not to, he knew he really ought not even to lay eyes on words like these. Although he knew them so well, imagining them on the page in his own microscopic handwriting produced a flutter of—what?—Nerves? Fear? An apprehension of power? Probably the last. The trouble with these outer covers had always been—as he had found in his own work—that the immediate impact of the image destroys thought. And yet, image is all.

The corn was orient, and immortal wheat, which never should be reaped and was never sown. I thought it had stood from everlasting to everlasting.

'Hot shit!' said Macphee, aloud.

One was here once again up against the romantic/classic dichotomy. Romantic imagery, relying always more upon its parts than upon its whole, tended to be more successful in short quotation; classic imagery required for its effect the quiet build-up of apparently unimportant detail before the meaningful resolution could strike home with its full force. As a result the bomb had an inherent—no, not weakness, he would not admit that—call it a 'danger factor'. In the wrong hands the detonators might go off without exploding the main charge. Macphee had to believe that this highly sensitive trigger mechanism was part of the bomb's power, but was aware that a badly timed or executed delivery could produce a half-cock result. This was one of his reasons for believing that a debate on the raising of the school leaving age was a suitable—as well as an inescapable—occasion for delivering the bomb. Such a debate must surely be conducted, he thought, at a suitably academic pace; and all the bomb needed, to start its chain reaction, was a modest amount of time.

59

Macphee, sitting at his table and stroking the outer surfaces of his bomb, was disturbed by a commotion outside his locked door. Now the door was being knocked upon, an unheard-of event in this quiet, discreet house. Macphee moved towards the door with something like murder in his heart, already suspecting the appalling truth.

It was Emrys Pugh, drunk, bearing bottles. Macphee stood in his doorway, arms spread to prevent entry.

'Go away,' he said, quietly and venomously.

'Go away? Are you mad? I track you down at last with sleuthful cunning to your disgusting little lair and by the holy Christ you tell me to *go away*! Look! Look! I have brought you beer. Vast, incredible quantities of seething alcohol! I come to you, you poor, insane, blind old bugger, with love in my heart and music on my lips and gifts in my hands and you tell me to go away! Get out of the fucking way, man!'

Pugh lurched forward and, as it seemed, passed through Macphee, who might not have been there for all the obstacle he presented. In the midst of his horror at this obscene incursion Macphee had time to muse weightily upon the fact that all Welsh poets, except those who were clergymen, had the same trivial act, but was unable, for the moment, to remember who had started it.

'Finished off your pomegranate, you greedy bastard,' said Pugh, turning mother and lover on their backs and scooping out the few remaining seeds with unclean fingernails. 'Where do you keep your tooth glass?'

Macphee had no tooth glass, no drinking-glass of any kind: he never drank except in public houses, nor out of opening hours.

'Emrys,' he said, pleading, 'you can't stay, you know. I mean—I can't have you here, in this room. It's quite impossible.'

'Damn, man, I'm here, aren't I?' said Pugh. 'Nothing's impossible. Look upon the living truth of it. I am *here*, me, Emrys Pugh, poet, of Penrhyndeudraeth, running my dirty fingers along the spines of your incredibly catholic collection of the World's Worst Verse, I'm unscrewing the cap from this huge flagon of foul fizzy ale, I'm about to apply the opening to my busy little mouth . . . Hamish, man, this is *real*, this is *happening*, here, now, your boozing companion of many a long evening is here in your nasty little womb all hot and drunk and disgusting and *alive*, Hamish, and there is abso-fucking-lutely no way you can pretend that matters are otherwise.'

'I'll kill you,' said, or thought, Macphee.

He contemplated such an act—which might indeed become necessary if Pugh could not be persuaded to leave quietly—with no emotion at all. If it could have been done, from where Macphee stood in the open doorway, by some such simple movement as pressing a button or pulling a lever, he would have done it now without pause for reflection. He could not let any agency obstruct the day's course of action. Already he had been intolerably disturbed and delayed by Pugh's incursion into his room. Macphee wished he could remember where the breadknife was.

'Look here, Emrys,' he said, in a reasonable and friendly tone. 'I have to change and go out, I don't have time . . .'

'Rubbish!' shouted Pugh. 'Man-diawl, time's the only bloody thing you *have* got, Hamish! I've never known a man who'd got so much time and so little to do with it!' Pugh glugged at his bottle, smacked froth from his mouth with the back of his hand, and grinned maliciously. 'Five years since your last slim volume, Hamish,' he taunted. 'Five years!'

It was a taunt Macphee could bear equally enough, knowing what he knew; and anyway he was not disposed to rise or in any other way respond.

'I have to change and go out,' he repeated doggedly, and started to unbutton his cardigan. Pugh then did a terrible thing. He picked up the bomb.

'Put that down, Emrys. Please.'

'Nice old binding. I've got a copy of *Childe Harold* almost identical. Published in Leipzig. No title on the spine either. What's this?'

Macphee found himself unable to move, almost unable to breathe. When he spoke, his voice cracked.

'You mustn't open it. You mustn't.'

Pugh opened it.

'OM,' he said, and laughed.

'Yahweh.' He laughed again. Pugh had a very loud laugh. It cascaded across the room, through the open door, and down the stairs.

'O Logos. What the hell . . . ?'

Pugh flipped over a few pages, shaking his head, chuckling. Oh where, where, *where* is that bloody breadknife? Macphee was demanding of his errant memory; but still could neither move nor speak.

'A motion and a spirit that impels . . . What the fuck is this, Hamish? A bloody golden treasury of the world's best loved quotations?'

'No,' Macphee heard himself say, 'it's a bomb.'

The act of speaking released him from his paralysis. He leapt with both hands for Pugh's throat, screaming. He would have been surprised to learn that he was screaming; he believed himself to be acting calmly and logically; taking regrettable but necessary action. He could see nothing and, for the moment, hear nothing; and he felt no pain from the blows Pugh was raining on his body. His thumbs had found Pugh's windpipe. He had only to hold on long enough, squeeze firmly enough, and all this physical commotion would cease, the unexpected obstacle would have been removed. He hoped that his glasses, which had fallen off, would not get broken, but knew that he could manage his approaching duties without them. His mind, as he thought of those duties, seemed to be working with great speed and clarity.

There came a point at which Pugh appeared to grow several more hands. Two of these were prising Macphee's fingers apart, two more were holding his shoulders in a steely grip. He was being shaken, then slammed against a wall, held there. Oh God, he thought, I'm going to fail. But I can't! I can't fail!

62

Someone was pushing his glasses on to his nose; with them, miraculously, sound, as well as some degree of sight, returned. He became aware that there were two large men in the room, one of them holding him against the wall, the other holding— or perhaps supporting—Pugh.

'That's it, Macphee,' said the man who was holding him, 'that bloody does it. You're finished here. You're going out, right now, understand?'

Pugh seemed to be sobbing. Macphee felt a need to explain. 'The bomb, you see, he was handling the bomb . . .'

'Shouting and screaming and brawling—lost us four customers, maybe more, they was scuttling out like rabbits . . . Well, that's bloody it. Can't think why you was let stay.'

'He could have set it off, you see,' said Macphee reasonably, 'could have started the fuses. It's dangerous.'

'Dangerous? Fuses? What fuses, for chrissakes?'

'On the bomb.'

'Bomb?' A slightly hysterical note had crept into the man's voice. He shouted at Pugh. 'Hey, you! What's he talking about?'

'That book,' said Pugh in—Macphee was interested to note—a strangled voice. 'He says it's a bomb. He's crazy.'

'It is a bomb,' said Macphee, with the lack of emphasis of one so certain of his fact that he doesn't even need to be believed. There was a small silence. Pugh coughed, and was abruptly sick.

'Oh Christ!' said the man who did the talking. 'Get him to the bathroom. Clean him up and throw him out. Now listen, Macphee, I don't believe that's a bomb, but I want it and you out of here pronto. Now. Go on—git!'

Macphee was given a shove, and found himself on his hands and knees with his face only a foot away from the bomb, where it lay on the floor between table and bed.

'Move!' said the man. 'Come on, Macphee! Move! Macphee picked up the bomb and wrapped his new shirt around it. The man thrust his stick and overcoat into his arms and pushed him towards the door.

'Out! Out! Go on—out! I'll put the rest of your gear out the back yard, and if I see your nose in this house again I'll bloody flatten it, understand?'

'Don't push,' said Macphee mildly, as he felt his way down the stairs. 'If I fall it might go off.'

The man began to swear through clenched teeth, obscenely, inventively, without end. Macphee realised he was frightened. Well, so he should be, so he should be. Everyone should be frightened. The house of cards was soon to fall about their ears.

From the bathroom on the landing came the sound of Pugh retching. Macphee felt a touch of—no, not remorse, for his attack had been essential, inevitable—of compassion. 'Look after him,' he said to the man behind him. 'It wasn't his fault. He didn't realise what he was doing. You see—it doesn't *look* like a bomb.'

'Out,' said the man. 'Out.'

In the street Macphee hung his new overcoat around his shoulders and set off carefully towards the public lavatory in Leicester Square. He felt serene and untouchable. The many bruises he had sustained during his brief bout of violence were now beginning to throb pleasantly, and his shoulders were stiff with the protests of ill-used muscle, but he knew that the faithful old body, which had carried him well enough for more years than he had wanted, would hold up for the last task. After that he would go elsewhere, let the body go back to its soil.

In the public lavatory Macphee changed into his stiff new shirt, hung the old one on the corner of a door for whoever might fancy it. It had been second or third hand when it came into Macphee's possession and was perhaps at the end of its useful life, like his bruised and declining body. Then worms shall try, he thought, thy long preserv'd virginity. A joke.

The knot of his tie, which had not been re-tied for years, was, he knew, greasy with dirt; but, without his magnifying glass, he could not undo it and find another, cleaner, area of cloth to display. The tie was important. It proclaimed him to be a sometime scholar of Eton College for Boys, and, although the claim was a lie, Macphee had faith in its power. He doubted whether the tie, if such existed, of Peebles Grammar School, would have the same calming effect on policemen.

Macphee decided to test his new overcoat, his new shirt, his Old Etonian tie on the policeman at the entrance to the House of Commons Strangers' Gallery as soon as possible.

The time was now, he was amazed to discover, still only a little after two-thirty—the House had only just commenced to sit. After Private Business, Question Time would last until three-thirty, and unknown business fill the time between then and the opening of the debate on the school leaving age at five. If he got in at the first attempt, Macphee thought, these hours could happily be spent in meditation, or in gloating over the perfection of the bomb. If his appearance provoked resistance he could wait for the officer on duty to be relieved—probably at four—and try again. Different policemen, he had observed, reacted to him in different ways.

In the event he had no trouble. It took him little more than half an hour to find his way to Parliament Square, feeling his way down Whitehall with the caution, he thought wryly, of a blind man who wishes to stay alive. A woman in a fur coat, moving in a cloud of some very resinous scent, held him closely beside her at the traffic lights, as if suspecting him of foolhardiness; when the lights changed she guided him across to the opposite pavement with exaggerated care, chattering brightly about the inadequacy of the social services. She said she had a particular interest in meths drinkers. Macphee didn't understand why she should advance this information. At the main entrance to the House a friendly young policeman showed Macphee how, by following the railings, he could find his way to the steps leading up to the Strangers' Gallery, where another officer, he was assured, would help him.

And so it proved. This policeman was of a type Macphee had encountered before, modelling himself on an avuncular image created by fiction, radio and television. Everything was a warm, bland, comfortable joke. 'I'm sure you won't mind, sir,' he said. 'Excuse me.' He felt under Macphee's armpits, down his legs, over his hips, and brought to light the bomb, which he opened. A cheque for £45 and a £5 note fluttered to the ground and were ignored.

'Superfetation of το εν,' the policeman read, or rather, saw.

'Poetry, eh?' he said in an interested voice. 'Matter of fact I'm a bit of a poet myself. We've got a literary club in my division. You'd be surprised, sir, some of the stuff we do.'

Macphee was sure he would be surprised, and at any other time he would have felt impelled to delve more deeply into this phenomenon. How sad, he thought. Too little, and too late.

The policeman put his foot on the £5 note, picked up the cheque, and handed it, and the bomb, back to Macphee. 'Some of them in there,' he said, nodding towards the House of Commons, 'could do with a dose of poetry.' Macphee had to agree. He smiled, nodded, and tapped carefully up the stone stairs. Seven hundred years, he thought, since Simon de Montfort's parliament. Amazing that it should have taken so long: between the formulation of one concept and the formulation of another, the big sleep.

Macphee sat by the rail in the Strangers' Gallery for two hours, half listening to the edgy, jocular and portentous voices that echoed around the space below. Occasionally he turned the pages of the bomb, but could not read, having been separated by events from his reading-glass. He had no need of sight, though; his head throbbed with words.

A poet soaring in the high reason of his fancies . . .

Macphee could have done with a drink, but was otherwise as happy, probably, as at any time in his life.

So was hire joly whistle well ywette, lucky pilgrim.

A nice line, but he hadn't put it in the bomb. He had had to curb in himself a tendency, noted at an early stage of construction, to fall back too readily on Chaucer when in need of the common touch, reminding himself that there were fewer and fewer people in the world who could hear the gorgeous rhythms correctly.

Macphee found himself thinking suddenly of the seething seeds inside the pomegranate. How very like a bomb that fruit was, bursting with potential power! And, as with his own bomb, only one seed need fall on fertile ground and . . . Ah, what a marvel!

Macphee thought briefly about Pugh. A poet, of a sort, but adrift in a language and a culture alien to his mother's knee. A man, therefore, forced to take up attitudes. Macphee felt a little sorry for him, but not much: the image of Pugh's dirty fingernails casually defiling the symbols of all Macphee had ever known of love was strong enough to justify Macphee's onslaught, even if he had never picked up and opened the bomb. But Macphee wished the man no harm. He had an outstanding memory for verse.

Now Macphee looked at the bomb in his hands. He was sorry it was not shaped like a pomegranate, but knew that this whimsy was the result of his having thought of it for so long as a bomb. It looked, in fact, like what it was, a manuscript book, a harmless enough object; but Macphee had no doubt about its deadliness.

At eight o'clock, after listening for some time to a government spokesman advancing reasons, which had nothing remotely to do with Value, for raising the school leaving age to seventeen, Macphee stood suddenly and, without tension, with no specific provocation, simply because he felt the time had come, tossed his bomb outwards towards the centre of the chamber. Only seconds after it had, presumably—for he could see nothing—reached the floor, Macphee's head exploded in stars, in searing white light. He felt himself falling sideways.

In the Press Gallery 'Bill' Maxwell awoke with a start to find his fellow journalists, like the Members of Parliament in the chamber below, fighting each other to get through the exits. Without knowing why, he joined them, crying, 'What's happening? For Christ's sake, what's happening?' But no one could, or would, tell him.

On the floor of the chamber the bomb seethed, unopened.

In the Strangers' Gallery, falling, as it seemed, very slowly sideways towards the floor, towards darkness, Macphee thought: The power of words! The power of w

Wrong Play

We had arranged to meet in the quieter of the two pubs favoured by Stratford's actors. Up the road, in the Dirty Duck, the swirling crush in the small side bar would have too much convivial energy in it to be suitable for a reunion. Walter would know too many of his fellow actors, and I, by now, too few, for us to find a satisfactory balance of communication among the simmering loves and hates, the busy cliques and feuds, in which we had once shared a delighted mutual interest. Rumour, painted full of tongues, had lost my ear.

I would in fact be enjoying three reunions this mellow summer evening. One, with Julie, would be after a separation of no great duration. She had been in my bed, in London, a week previously. I would be in hers, I trusted, this night in Stratford. The reunion with Walter would have more novelty to it. I hadn't seen him for nearly five years, not since, in fact, we had last worked together, with me carrying a spear, Walter giving his Scroop, in *Henry IV ii*. Oddly enough, Walter was rehearsing the same play now, with a different director, a different part. Our friendship had survived, to some extent, because we both enjoyed writing letters: we consciously conducted, in fact, an old-fashioned correspondence. So I knew, even without gossip from Julie (delighted with herself at having landed Doll Tear-sheet) that Walter was haunted by the memory of Roy Dotrice's Justice Shallow in the Hall/Barton histories cycle of the 1960s. I also

71

knew that Walter would come through with a Shallow original enough for comparison to be irrelevant.

Had I been asked, at that moment, I might have said that the emotional impact of seeing Walter again would be at about the same level as that of seeing Julie again. I knew that I loved Julie at least as much as, probably more than, any other woman I had lived with, and the relationship had gone on so long by now as to have acquired, at least in the eyes of others, the status of marriage; although I think Julie had as much difficulty as I in thinking of ourselves as the marrying kind. However, I did love her; but though I didn't want to go to bed with him, I loved Walter just as much. It's this kind of thought that gives the idea of marriage an edge it ought not to have.

The third reunion, and the one which took place first, was with Rodney, once a fellow spear-carrier, subsequently, unlike me, a steadily rising pillar of the company and now about to make a further mark as Ancient Pistol (doubling, as it happens, as Rumour—but no one ever made a mark as Rumour). Our friendship was based, as far as I could see, on little more than my ability to make Rodney laugh, and my love of listening to his pealing laughter. We hadn't much else in common: he was all actor, I was not. Yet our relationship was based on the parts we played to each other.

I was sitting at the very end of the Long Bar in the Avon, sipping a demure lager (thoughts of later bedroom activity in mind) and sneering at the fuzzy photographs in the *Guardian*— does nobody teach these people the Laws of Contrast?—when Rodney came driving down the room on his powerful stocky legs. I pretended not to see him until he was upon me, crying, 'Great to see you, old mate!' and gripping my shoulder with strong fingers. I looked up.

'Good God! Rod!' I said. 'What? Still alive after the Third Bottle?'

Rodney smacked his forehead with the heel of his hand. 'Great Christ, yes! The Third Bottle. You bloody near did kill me, old mate, I promise you!'

'Had to finish the fourth on my tod,' I said, affecting grumpiness at the memory. It wasn't true, of course. I doubt if, on that night in London a couple of months before when we'd talked out the dawn, we even finished the second bottle—no great consumption, over a longish period, for two habitual whisky drinkers. Yet Rodney now rocked back on his heels as if in astonished admiration.

'I was out of it, was I? You put me under the table again?'

'You put yourself, Rod.'

'Oh, Cliff, mate, you're a wild man!' And Rodney put back his head and roared with laughter as if I'd made a fine joke.

That was how we were with each other. Schoolboyish, I don't deny it. Yet we had our moments of truth, all the more valuable, in some ways, for being embedded in acres of puppy play. We had recently discussed reasons why he was making it as an actor, while I was not. Rodney could easily have evaded so potentially fraught a subject, pretended, as so many did to themselves, that all I needed was 'the right chance'. But Rodney grinned, spread wide the fingers of both hands as if holding out to me a large heavy gift, and said, 'Jesus, old mate, you never even carried a spear with conviction. You wanted to know why you were carrying it. That never bothered me. Come hither. Go yonder. I come. I go. No thinking required.'

'I needed to know why I was facing in one direction rather than the other.'

'If an actor needs reasons, old mate, he has to make them up for himself, not wait to be told.'

'I never believed my own reasons.'

'That's just it. That famous detachment of yours—I've never known anyone so determined to remove himself from whatever scene he's in. It may be what makes you such a fucking good photographer but it was bloody fatal to you as an actor.'

Maybe Rodney wouldn't have spoken so openly if he hadn't known that I was already successful in my 'second profession' as a portrait photographer, but I doubt it. There was always an element of danger in talking seriously with him.

'What's this gnat's piss you're drinking?' he asked me now, widening his eyes at my lager. I explained the need for caution. It could become a long evening, I didn't want it to end badly. 'I'm waiting,' I told him, 'for a fair hot wench in flame-coloured taffata.'

'Wrong play,' said Rodney. 'Don't confuse me. You speak of Julie, though I make doubt about the taffata. Word around here is that you and Julie are through.'

What was this? What was this? My head spun. Rodney hadn't spoken out of turn, he was right there within our convention. What was alarming was his surprise that this was news to me. It could only, I reasoned, have come from Julie, unless . . .

'Someone been making claims?' I asked.

'Not a soul, that I know of.'

'Level with me, Rod.'

'Julie hasn't said a word, if that's what you mean. Stuff in the air, that's all. You know what it's like.'

I did know. I'd had my name linked, in the Dirty Duck, with the latest star-from-RADA before we'd even met. I'd also had my deepest secrets revealed as common knowledge. Seeing Rodney now embarrassed, I said, 'Rumour doth double, like the voice and echo, the number of the feared.'

'That's about it, old mate. Sorry.' He added, 'Right play, by the way.'

'I wouldn't know.'

'No. You don't have to.'

'Anything else?'

'No. I swear to God, old mate, I thought I was just up with the news—and bloody sad to hear it, too, make no mistake. It's all balls then, is it?'

'As far as I know, as of last Thursday.'

'Well, good, then. Let's have a Scotch.'

As of last Thursday, though, now I came or was forced to think about it, my relationship with Julie may indeed have undergone some slight modification. I was not sure. But it was nothing she would have relayed to anyone at Stratford, nor, if she did decide she wanted to be rid of me, would she go about it by dropping hints into the company's rumour-mill. She wasn't that kind of operator.

Anyway, I busily told myself, what had been said after our love-making last Thursday night wasn't even new, as far as subject-matter was concerned. It revolved around the unusual circumstance of our both having a whole weekend completely free of commitments. Relaxed, satisfied with the way our loving had gone, I had begun drowsily to outline the small treats that I had on offer to fill our two whole long days together—a drive out to Samuel Palmer's beautiful Shoreham valley in Kent, a pub lunch, a walk on the North Downs, a visit to some quaint young friends who were spending their parents' money on pretending to be subsistence farmers—when Julie suddenly put her hands over her ears. 'Sorry,' she said, 'sorry, sorry, no, I've been meaning to tell you, I can't. Sorry.'

'But you can. You know you can, darling. What's happened?'

'Nothing's happened. There's just something I've got to do.'

'So something has happened. There wasn't anything you'd got to do last time we spoke about this weekend.'

'I know. Sorry.'

There was a pause while I waited for her to tell me what had come up, and I felt the pause fill with an intransigent atmosphere which told me that Julie knew I wasn't going to like what she had to tell me, but that it would be a waste of her time and mine to argue about it.

'Well, aren't you going to tell me?'

She told me in a rush. 'I have to go to the Women's Peace Camp tomorrow. Three nights—Friday, Saturday, Sunday. I'll go straight on to Stratford early Monday morning.'

'You have to go?'

'I've said I would.'

'You were asked to?'

'No. I asked if I might. I'm sorry. It's something I've been meaning to do. And it's so little, nothing really, just a gesture. But I have to make it. Sorry.'

'Julie, darling . . .'

'You won't talk me out of it.'

'I know that. But couldn't you, just occasionally, give yourself a break? There are other people, you know, you don't have to reform the world single-handed. Anyway, you're not one of the Peace Camp women. They make their point by being there all the time.'

That stupid remark slipped out without due care and attention.

'I'd be one of them if I could. If I had the support. I think they're wonderful. And far more effective than anything I've ever done.'

'If you had the support. Do you mean, from me?'

Julie laughed, but not on a note that gave me any pleasure.

'That'd be the day!'

'Oh God, we've been through all this before.'

'I'll say we have. I can't think how we put up with each other.'

I wanted this to de-escalate. I scratched her between her shoulder blades. That went down well.

'Julie, sweetheart, you know very well that your commitment is one of the things I love about you. You're a fierce little battler, and I admire you for it. But you can't ask me to be what I'm not, to say I believe something when half my mind will always doubt it.'

'Up a bit. There. No, a bit to the right. There. Now stop. Thanks. Well, all I can say is, you're going to have to make up your mind about something one of these days or you'll never grow up.'

That was a gift. I'd been waiting for years for someone to say that to me. 'The only way of strengthening one's intellect,' I told her, 'is to make up one's mind about nothing.'

'That's cheap!'

'It doesn't come from a cheap source.'

'Oh God, you and your squirrel mind! Who?'

'John Keats.'

'But it's ridiculous!'

'Far from it. Something every poet knows. Let the mind be a thoroughfare for *all* thoughts, sayeth our Jack.'

'It's balls, Keats or no Keats.'

'It's me, Julie or no Julie.'

That, once it was out, sounded horribly dangerous, but oddly enough it made her smile.

Anyway, that was it. Goodnight kisses followed, and calm sleep. We even had another quick fuck the next morning before I went off to the studio. You can't call that a quarrel. Yet when Rodney came back from the bar with two huge whiskies in his clean blunt fingers he said, 'Sorry to be so long. I got nobbled by that hairy arsehole Larry Instone. Know what he said? He took a look down the room at you and said, "Well, Rod, I guess you'll be making an early bid for Julie Timberlake now she's free." '

A goose walked over my grave.

'What did you say?'

'Told him to get stuffed. Told him Julie wasn't free. Told him that if I heard of him making a pass at her I would personally see to it that he hung himself in his own heir apparent garters.'

'Thanks. Wrong play.'

'Yes, but right sentiment don't you think? Hey ho, here they come.'

Perhaps I should have said that I'd be enjoying four reunions, for Selina, Walter's lady, is very much a somebody in her own right, a long way from being just an appendage of Walter's. I'll describe her as she came swanning through the light press of people around the entrance to the Long Bar, leading, as always, her little caravan: approaching seventy, at a hazardous guess; enveloped in a vast, highly decorated gown; a monocle in one eye, ready to be dropped in astonishment on its black silk ribbon; a long thin cigar clamped between her widely spaced teeth; a fine curtain of straight black hair obscuring one side of her face . . . the overall impression one of watching a galleon sail with conscious grandeur across a harbour full of lesser craft. It was flattering to know that her point of docking would be at my side.

Walter came into the bar several yards behind Selina, with an arm around Julie's shoulders, his head bent close to hers, hurriedly trying to finish some comic anecdote before reaching other company. I was smiling already, just at the sight of them all.

What Walter found in me to nurture our loving friendship I can't easily fathom. There is a thirty year age difference between us—he was playing Romeo, here in Stratford, a decade before I was born—but nothing remotely like a 'generation gap' had ever disturbed us. When we first met we did discover that we had one distinct thing in common. Unlike most actors we each had a dedicated interest outside the theatre: I my photography, Walter his painting, which was unquestionably of a professional standard. 'A man of parts,' as Rodney once said, adding with lewd admiration, 'and very *active* parts, I do assure you, unbelievably active, for any age.'

Julie, though listening with proper lip-twitching attention to Walter's anecdote, had already seen me, and acknowledged me with a dip of the head towards Walter which said, as plainly as if she'd shouted it at me, 'Wants to finish his story—I'll let him.' Then she pushed back against Walter's arm, slowing him to a stop in the middle of the room, holding him there while he finished his story. She wouldn't let our own greeting, nor Walter's punchline, be spoiled by having them clash.

Then Selina was upon me, arms flung wide for a great hug. 'Cliff, *darling*, how absolutely *gorgeous!*' We kissed, and made delighted loving noises, while Rodney stood off, arms folded, grinning, like a small boy whose promised treat was coming true. Selina skipped aside and pushed me towards Walter, now hurrying to join us.

'My dear fellow!' said Walter. We hugged and kissed, a convention common enough in men of my generation, unusual,

I'd have thought, in Walter's, and somehow typical of his unthinking generosity. Julie, when Walter released me, slipped her hand into mine and squeezed it. I was grateful for the gesture; and noted, not without a twinge of irritation, that Rodney, Walter and Selina had all registered it, unexceptional as it was.

For an hour or so, over our assorted drinks, we swapped news of mutual friends, memories of past adventures, plans for the future. I asked Walter if he'd got Justice Shallow by the tail. Rodney snorted with sudden laughter.

'He's for all the world like a forked radish . . . he's the very genius of famine, yet . . .'

Selina, hawking with laughter, supplied, 'Yet lecherous as a monkey!' We all fell about, and Julie, beside me, squeezed my arm.

'Shallow's a gift,' said Walter, 'to an old ham with a failing memory. He says everything twice or three times. So when I can't remember the next line I keep going by saying the one I've just said, the one I've just said, Oh yes, the one I've just said.'

Julie squeezed my arm again, and the squeeze said, dear old Walter, what a joy to be with! and I nudged her, and my nudge said, I know you think he's sexy too. This was all good normal wordless conversation between Julie and me. I couldn't believe that there was anything seriously wrong. In fact she looked and sounded, after her weekend with the Peace Camp women, poised and self-confident. If there was a flicker of concern as her eyes darted with pleasure among her companions it might well be, I thought, a sense that I might be feeling, as I was, not quite as much a true part of the Stratford scene as once I had been.

'Got to go,' said Rodney suddenly, standing. 'Seven o'clock wig-fitting. Scandalous. I shall sneak to Equity, then they'll catch it.'

'You won't,' said Julie, herself an active left-wing member of the union, 'you don't give a bone button about Equity.'

'Too right,' said Rodney equably. ' 'Tis no sin for a man to labour in his profession.'

'Wrong play!' said Julie smartly, too delighted with her own sharpness of memory to engage Rodney further about Equity.

'Right. But now listen,' said Rodney, addressing me. 'Urgent final message. There's a circus. It's in a field near Hampton Lucy, quarter of an hour's drive, Walter knows where. You've got to see it. I don't know whether you like circuses or not, but this one's different, it's got to be seen. There's a show at seven thirty, you can be back here boozing by eight fifteen—in fact I'll meet you here and we'll all go for a meal. I won't tell you more. Just do it. Oh, and Cliff—take your camera.'

'It was when we were on tour with the Scottish play and—oh shit, what was it?'

'*Ghosts*, of course, you silly old dope!' Selina supplied. 'Rodney giving his Oswald.'

'That's right. Rod's first lead. And Macduffing in the Scottish play, wasn't he? Anyway, Selly came up to see us in Durham, of all places . . .'

'An absolutely *vile* dump, not the town of course, that's rather a fun place, but the theatre, my darlings, the dressing rooms! You couldn't swing a mouse let alone a cat, but anyway, Walter and Rodney decided . . .'

'Shut the fuck up, Selly, I'm telling this . . .'

Walter and Selina always conducted their stories like this, in tandem, and however often Walter shut Selina up she always bounced back in again, often with, 'Oh, Walter, you bastard, let *me* tell it, let *me*, this is *my* bit, you selfish old sod!' If I'd been Walter it would have driven me mad, but to the uninvolved listener it was great entertainment.

Selina was driving, her long thin cigar waggling up and down at an amazing speed whenever she managed to chip into Walter's complex story. Sitting in the back, holding hands with Julie, I felt numb with pleasure. Whatever Rumour said, Julie's hand said otherwise. I wasn't listening to the anecdote with much attention, but was glad to have the two animated voices washing over me. The lush Warwickshire countryside was bathed in golden evening sunlight. We were approaching an event which could ask nothing of me but appreciation.

Then Julie whispered, 'Listen, darling, we have to have a pow-wow, soon as poss.'

'Not easy.'

'We have to.'

'After dinner?'

'Before.'

'I don't understand.'

'Nor do I. That's why.'

'Okay. We'll look for a moment.'

'Thanks.'

'. . . and Rod came on,' said Walter, his story still in full flow, 'drunk as a lord, but you'd never have known. Upright and steady. Costume more or less okay, wig and make-up normal, every inch a Macduff. A real pro', I thought to myself. And then he said . . . then he said . . . Oh, shit, what the fuck did he say, Selly?'

'I can't remember,' said Selina, already laughing at what should have been the punchline but which escaped them both, 'but it wasn't Macduff, it was that little shit Oswald!'

We all dissolved in laughter. It was a good anecdote, even only half heard, even with its punchline blurred by a lapse of memory, and Julie gave my hand a squeeze that told me she wasn't totally preoccupied with whatever the substance of our 'pow-wow' was to be.

No other cars were parked beside the road near the gate into the field where the circus's 'big top' had been erected. Like the village of Hampton Lucy itself, through which we'd just passed, the field seemed deserted. Hanging on the gate was a bruised sign announcing, in once bright letters edged with multi-coloured balls, 'SPROAT's CIRCUS, E. J. Sproat, *prop*.' The time of today's shows were given as 4.30 and 7.30, prices of admission as 'Best Seats 7/6d., Seats 5/-, Children 3/6d.' No decimalisation for E. J. Sproat.

'Doesn't look as if anything's going on,' said Julie doubtfully.

'Well, darlings, it's after half past seven, so there ought to be,' said Selina. 'Let's go and look.'

The Big Top—in fact a very little top—was on the far side of the field, an old caravan parked beside it, the back of a lorry partly integrated into the tent. When we were half way across the field we began to hear the slow poppety-pop of an idling generator, and smiled encouragingly at each other: something was happening over there. The long walk across the field seemed to go on and on. I wanted to talk to Julie, but here I was, going to the circus. There was nothing to be done. Swing with it, I told myself. Julie, it seems, had told herself the same. 'Oh look,' she said eagerly, tugging at my sleeve, 'there's someone . . .'

The tiny figure of a woman clad in tights, a tutu, and a tinsel-trimmed bodice had darted across the grass between the tent and the caravan, disappearing behind the caravan and appearing a moment later at an open window in its side. We now saw that above this window was a notice saying, 'Circus Box Office, E. J. Sproat, prop.' We altered course towards it.

'You're a bit late, duckies,' cried the woman in the window with a beaming smile that revealed a few very small teeth. 'The show's half over. But never mind, never mind, you're here, that's what matters. Actors, aren't you?'

This was startling. None of us had yet spoken. Among us, only Selina, in her long gown, was at all unconventionally dressed. Walter, in my eyes, looked like a retired colonel or a well-heeled country gent. I wore my generation's uniform of jeans, T-shirt, and short denim jacket. Julie also wore jeans, with a dark blue cashmere sweater, which I liked because it revealed her pointy little nipples. We certainly weren't a showy crowd.

'You've got our number, I'm afraid,' said Walter, grinning up at her.

'Oh, I can always tell. I can smell the grease paint.'

She can only have been speaking metaphorically, for her own face was plastered with enough of the stuff to have obscured any

82

traces that might linger, not evident to me, about Julie and Walter. We were now close enough to see that our tiny sequined and tinselled box-office lady was certainly not under seventy years old. Although Walter was well into his seventies, he appeared a youth beside her.

I looked at Julie. Something very like beatific adoration was in her face. She gazed up at the wrinkled, painted face in the caravan window.

'We've come to the circus,' she said, like a child.

'Of course you have, darling, of *course* you have, and so you shall. I'm Ma Sproat. My son's on now. He's got some beautiful acts, you'll love him. Sonny, I call him. It's always Sonny and Ma.'

Walter proffered two pounds. 'Best Seats, please,' he said.

'Half price for actors,' said Ma Sprout, rummaging in a drawer below the window. 'Rule of the show, always has been. Half price for the profession.'

'Rubbish!' said Walter firmly. 'We're all in work.'

'Are you?' marvelled Ma Sproat. 'All of you? All in work? Isn't that *marvellous*, my dears! I'm so happy for you. And I'll tell you what. I'll give you Best Seats at Seat prices! There!'

She gave Walter back one of his pound notes.

As we followed Ma Sproat from the caravan towards a loose flap in the tent's wall I heard Selina, behind me, whisper fiercely to Walter, '*You shouldn't have taken that quid back you mean old sod!*'

'Don't be daft, Selly darling,' said Walter.

Ma Sproat, with much ceremony, showed us to Best Seats: a row of eight or ten stacking chairs with lightly upholstered seats, facing the focal point of the ring: the little tent-within-a-tent from which all entrances and exits were made. On either side of Best Seats three untiered rows of wooden benches curved round the ring's perimeter. These were Seats, 5/-, Children 3/6d. Apart from ourselves there were no adults in the audience. I estimated that, in theatre terms, and including Walter's pound, there was no more than £8.50 in the house.

There was a stir among the children, and a flutter of whispering, as we took our seats. But in a moment all was quiet again, all eyes intent on the magic in the ring. Sonny Sproat, a man in his forties with a long, sad, withdrawn face, was slowly twirling a very small lariat a few inches above the canvas floor of the ring. He was dressed in cowboy clothes and stood with his studded high-heeled boots wide apart, the small circle of the lariat spinning between them. Sonny watched it intently, as if it had a life of its own. I wondered what on earth he was going to do with such a small circle of rope until it dawned on me that he wasn't going to do anything more with it than he was already doing. He knew his audience better than I did. I could tell, from the silent, absorbed faces of the children, that watching a cowboy twirling a rope, inside a ring, inside a tent, was magic enough.

'For my next act,' said Sonny, in a surprisingly deep voice, as he let his lariat come to rest at his feet, 'I need three volunteers—you, you and you!'

Howls of laughter from the children. The three blushing boys Sonny had pointed at were thrust into the ring by their giggling neighbours. Sonny arranged them back to back in a triangle, picked up a larger lariat, got it moving, then raised his arm high above the boys' heads and slowly brought the spinning circle of rope down over the three excited, fearful little bodies, up again over their heads, down around them again, lower and lower, until, with a puff of dust, the rope came to rest on the canvas at their feet. Dazed and delighted, the three boys scampered for their seats. There was a patter of applause in which we, with our louder hands, enthusiastically joined.

I looked sideways at Julie. Without turning her head she said, in a strangled voice, 'Don't look at me.'

I looked at Selina on my other side. She waggled an unlit cigar at me and whispered, 'Bit bloody cry-making, all this.' Beyond her Walter was blowing his nose into a large red handkerchief.

Ma Sproat, in what looked like a star-spangled dressing

gown, came on with two little dogs for the next act. The dogs—some sort of terrier I think—pranced and danced and sat and begged and chased each other in circles to order. They weren't all that well trained but the children loved them, and again the climax of the act involved the participation of the audience: a pair of girls and a pair of boys held up tissue-paper-covered hoops for the dogs to jump through. Then Sonny was on again, in ring-master's top hat and scarlet tails, with a cracking whip and a bright little pony which cantered, with much showy head-tossing, round and round the ring. The children cheered.

'Show me,' cried out Sonny suddenly, 'show me a little girl who eats more sweets than are good for her.'

The whip cracked. The pony slowed, looking at the children with its head on one side. The whip cracked twice, and the pony curtsied before a plump little girl on one of the front benches. Not surprisingly she didn't see the funny side of it, and burst into tears. Her delighted neighbours comforted her. The pony trotted on. 'Show me a little boy who never runs away.' The boy the pony curtsied before stood up on his bench and thumped his chest proudly. 'Show me a man who likes kissing other men's wives.' The pony trotted round and curtsied in front of me.

I did, 'Oh my God all is discovered.' Julie did, 'I always suspected and now I know and I'm not speaking to *you* again.' I turned away from Julie and kissed Selina. She did, 'Ah bliss, what bliss!' and Walter did, 'I'll settle up with you later!' and we all got a round of applause.

After the pony Ma Sproat came on briefly, dressed now in diamante tights, yellowing muslin tutu and sequin-covered bodice. Muffled circus music came from the little tent while Ma did a funny little dance, all twirls and leaps, half way between ballet and ballroom dancing. It had probably once had some nimble acrobatic feats choreographed into its pattern, which advancing age had forced Ma to jettison. She did in fact at one point attempt a spin but had to turn it into a sideways leap as she lost balance. Although moving, on this account, to us adults, the dance didn't really amount to much until Ma plucked a very fat boy out of the audience and made him partner her, which was amazingly funny and good, the fat boy so serious about his embarrassing task, the old circus lady so tender and sensitive with her guidance and praise.

Then Sonny was back, in clown's pantaloons, a bright red ping-pong ball on his nose, tripping over his long flapping feet as he pushed a triangular metal frame across the canvas. Ma Sproat, releasing the fat boy, continued her weird dance. Sonny disappeared into the tent again and suddenly the music stopped, and Ma's dance with it. She flung out her arms for applause, and got it. Sonny reappeared again, pushing another triangular frame which he edged into position opposite the first.

'What would you get,' said Ma Sproat very slowly, as if she really needed to know, 'if you crossed an elephant with a kangaroo?'

'I don't know,' said Sonny, also very slowly, and without ceasing to work on positioning the two triangular frames. 'What would you get if you crossed an elephant with a kangaroo?'

'Holes all over Australia,' said Ma Sproat.

Sonny laughed so much that he got his legs entangled with each other and fell flat on his face. The children roared. Ma had picked up a thin steel wire rope with a ring spliced into one end of it. She slipped this ring around a hook that poked up through the canvas. Sonny was busy threading the rest of the wire through the apexes of the metal frames. While they did this Ma Sproat asked, 'What did the big chimney pot say to the little chimney pot?'

'I don't know,' said Sonny, as he pulled the wire taught and secured his end of it to a hook that protruded from the side of the little tent. 'What did the big chimney pot say to the little chimney pot?'

'You're too young to smoke,' said Ma Sproat.

Sonny went into convulsions again and ended up on his back,

the long floppy toes of his clown's boots quivering absurdly in the air. It was his pratfalls the children loved, rather than the jokes that occasioned them—one could tell from their whispering that they were all perfectly familiar with these old chestnuts, and no doubt Sonny was aware that this was part of the pleasure they gave.

Ma Sproat had disappeared into the little tent. Sonny, busy screwing up some device beside the tent that further tightened the wire between its anchors, called out to the children, 'Why was the tomato blushing?'

The children murmured among themselves, and then a bold girl, giggling self-consciously, called back, 'Because it saw the salad dressing!'

Sonny staggered around the ring, clutching his stomach, stumbling and tripping, doubling up and arching backwards, until he walked smack into the big top's centre pole and knocked himself out. He lay there, spreadeagled, while the children hawked and whooped with delight; and then suddenly, in an amazingly athletic movement, somersaulted to his feet, stuck an arm and a commanding finger into the air and cried out, like a herald's trumpet, 'Pah-pah pah-*pah*! Pah-pa-pa-pa-*pah*! My lords and ladies, ladies and gentlemen, boys and girls, dogs, cats and *mice*! Let me have your attention! For the great! the only! the indescribably brave, beautiful and graceful, the peak the crest and the summit of this and every evening, the one and only . . . Signorita . . . Spaghetti!'

From the little tent more scratchy circus music welled up, louder than before. Ma Sproat came out soberly. She had added a feather boa to her sequined costume, and carried a split-cane parasol, vaguely Chinese in flavour. She tripped lightly towards the frame furthest away from the audience, where Sonny was now standing, his hands cupped to form a step. Ma put a slippered foot into the cup and was hoisted up to what could now be identified as two footsteps at the apex of the frame. Gingerly she slid a foot out on to the wire, testing it. She raised her parasol. The other foot came out quickly behind the first, crossing the wire at right angles to it. She advanced slowly along the wire.

She was only perhaps five feet above the ground, but a fall would surely have broken her brittle old bones. Apart from the distant, grinding music there was utter silence. Sonny lurked below, near the wire, ready, I hoped, to catch his mother if she fell. The wire sagged as she reached the centre, where she did a little turn and return, the merest gesture of a dance. Now Sonny threw a red silk scarf over the wire. Ma Sproat, one foot raised behind her for balance, the parasol wavering above her head, bent and retrieved it with her ancient teeth.

As we all wildly applauded I looked across at Julie again. She was smiling broadly, clapping like mad. Tears were streaming down her cheeks.

My heart turned over. That's the right, the accurate phrase, but it leaves so much out: the pain, the awful sense of weakness, of vulnerability, both hers and mine. I had never felt anything remotely like this, for her or for anyone else, however often I may have told women that I loved them. It was as if all her parts, physical and mental, spiritual too although Julie would reject the word, had suddenly become visible to me both separately and as the substance of this cohering whole. While still clapping, I could feel myself trembling with the effort, the physical effort, of forcing myself to stay in my chair. It didn't last long, at that intensity, thank God. But I certainly didn't notice how, or even when, the show ended.

After the show we hung back, letting the excited, chattering children stream past us, until Ma Sproat could bring up and introduce Sonny. We said we were all with the Royal Shakespeare Company at Stratford—it seemed the simplest thing to do. Ma Sproat was cheerful, Sonny was dour.

'Do you know, we took over twelve quid at the tea-time show!' said Ma. 'Not bad. Always do better at tea-time, of course. They come on straight from school, a real crowd. In the evening, these days, most of them are home watching the telly. And parents don't come out the way they did. Get rid of the kids, that's the idea. But kids is what we're for, really. Apart from people like you.'

Sonny said, 'Dad would have curled up to see this.'

'Any circus is better than no circus Ernie always used to say,' said Ma stoutly.

'We aren't what we were,' said Sonny.

We proffered elaborate compliments, told them how much it had meant to us to see real, live, personal circus. Ma lapped it up, Sonny remained glum, withdrawn. 'He worries about our field,' Ma Sproat explained. 'Sonny was always a worrier.' Pressed, by Walter, to elaborate, she told us that the field in Hertfordshire which they owned, and where they wintered, had had a row of bungalows built beside it and the local council was now saying that, for obscure reasons of hygiene, the circus could no longer camp in its own field. 'It's difficult,' said Ma Sproat. 'We can't understand all their bits of paper. Of course, I always believe everything's going to work out all right—you have to, don't you, in the profession?—but Sonny thinks it's hopeless.'

'We're finished,' said Sonny, without much interest, 'if we can't winter in our field.' It was clear he hadn't much interest in us either. To him, we were salaried people, slumming. When we left we all kissed Ma Sproat. She loved that. Nobody, it was clear, was going to force unwanted kisses, or even handshakes, on Sonny.

Out in the field we all just looked at each other, shaking our heads in wonder, saying nothing. Well, Walter did say, 'Well, bless my boots!' which would do for all of us for the time being. We hadn't gone far across the field when Julie said, 'Hold on a sec',' and darted back into the big top. Selina pointed her cigar at me accusingly. 'You didn't take any photographs,' she said.

'I didn't, did I?'

'Not your sort of thing?'

'Not today, anyway.'

'Cagey young bugger, aren't you?' said Selina, with a friendly smile. Walter, as so often, leapt to my defence.

'Leave the lad alone, Selly, can't you? He knows what he wants to snap and what he doesn't want to snap.'

'But he's not going to tell anyone, is he?'

I grinned at her, shrugged, and wandered back a little way towards the big top. Julie reappeared, clutching a scrap of paper.

'Collecting autographs?' I called. As I said it I thought, have you gone crazy? what sort of stupid question is that? I felt I was going out of control.

Julie looked down at her piece of paper as she came slowly towards me, then waved it at me before tucking it away in her handbag.

'I got the address of their Hertfordshire place,' she said quietly as she arrived beside me. 'We're going to do something about that.'

'Are we?' It was supposed to come out hopeful but came out cynical. I couldn't do a thing right.

'Well, I am, anyway.'

We walked in silence to where Walter and Selina were standing. They were looking at us with worried curiosity. Something is taking its course, I thought vaguely.

'I got the address of their Hertfordshire place,' Julie told Walter and Selina, patting her handbag.

'Oh, well done, Julie, well done!' cried Walter.

'Brill, darling,' said Selina. 'We must do something about that, mustn't we, Cliff?'

Before I could answer—not that I had an answer easily to hand—Julie's eyes lighted on my unused Hasselblad. I saw them widen, knew what she was going to say, then she said it.

'Cliff!' she said. 'You didn't take any photos!'

'No.'

'Leave it, Julie,' advised Walter. 'We've been into that.'

'Not very *deep* into it, darling,' said Selina. 'A quick dip of the big toe, like silly Selly at the seaside, then out again quick as you like.'

'Shut the fuck up, Selly darling,' said Walter quietly.

90

Julie looked from Selina's face to mine. We were both grinning. She could make nothing of it.

'Old Selly was blubbing like a babe in there,' said Walter adroitly.

'So was I,' said Julie.

'So was Walter,' said Selina. 'Weren't you, darling? Go on, you know you were, you silly old fool.'

Walter nodded happily, and winked at me. Perhaps he was acknowledging that his change of subject had possibly not been as adroit as he had hoped. If so, he was right.

'Cliff wasn't, were you, Cliff?' said Julie.

'Nope. No snaps, no tears. Morgan the heartless monster, that's me.'

'Oh balls,' said Walter impatiently. I caught a glint in Julie's eye that I couldn't interpret, and then Selina had grabbed my arm, hugging it warmly, pulling me away. 'Nothing heartless about my boy Morgan,' she told the world, and marched me firmly across the field towards her car. As soon as we were out of Julie's hearing—if, indeed, we were; Selina didn't look back to make sure—she shook my arm fiercely and hissed, 'Honestly, Cliff darling, I ought to talk to you like a Dutch uncle, or a Dutch aunt if there is such a thing.'

'You don't want to believe everything you hear, Selly.'

'I should fucking hope so. Walter will never forgive you if you foul up over Julie. He's mad about her. Think's she's the best actress he's ever etcetera, straightest character he's ever etcetera, thinks in fact she's the cat's priceless bloody whiskers.'

'So do I.'

'Then why the hell do you . . . why don't you . . . ?' She shrugged, squeezed my arm, and said a brief, 'Sorry.'

'I yam what I yam, Selly,' I told her, trying to convey that I wasn't particularly pleased with this arrangement.

'You're a creature from fucking outer space, that's what you are darling.'

Rodney was waiting for us on the same seat at the end of the
Long Bar when we got back to the Avon. I had been so engaged,
on the drive back to Stratford, with the struggle not to throw
myself upon Julie and devour her, in public, body and soul, that
I'd forgotten that it was Rodney's idea that we should go to the
circus.

'See what I mean, old mate,' he said to me, tapping my
camera. 'I hope you got some good snaps. You could make a
brilliant feature story out of that.'

'Wake not the sleeping wolf,' said Walter.

'To wake a wolf is as bad as to smell a fox,' said Julie.

'I smell a fox,' said Rodney.

'I didn't take any snaps,' I said. 'There's your fox, Rod.'

'It stinks, too. Why not?'

I hesitated. He deserved some sort of answer, but I couldn't
very well tell him the truth, not here and now, with Julie
looking at me with an expression half way between curiosity
and amusement.

'My mind was on higher things,' I said.

'I'll believe that about anyone but you, old mate. A fast buck
followed by a fast f . . .'

'Rodney!' cried Selina, as if utterly scandalised. Everyone
laughed. Not for the first time, Rodney had defused a situation
with a piece of calculated insensitivity. 'Come on, darlings, for
Christ's sake, let's get some booze.'

So we had some booze, and discussed where we'd dine, and
made a decision, and Rodney made the phone call, and we
talked about the circus in a light way, and fell about quite a
lot. There were things to be said about the circus that would be
said on other occasions. Then Julie, rather tensely, and at a
wholly inappropriate moment, said, 'Listen, folks, I'm sorry,
but I've got to have a private word in this photographer's ear
before dinner. Can you give us ten minutes? We'll be over
there.'

'What! Shall we have incision?' said Rodney. 'Shall we
imbrue?'

'No imbruing, I promise,' said Julie. 'I'll bring him back in one piece.'

'Ten minutes, twenty, it's all one to us,' said Walter, 'no offence taken.'

'I'll so offend,' said Julie, 'to make offence a skill.'

'Wrong play!' we all shouted at her. That helped; but even so I felt a bit self-conscious as Julie and I walked across the room to an empty table. I imagine she did too.

'Go on, then,' I said, when we were seated. 'Pow-wow me.'

Julie looked both shifty and determined. I loved both expressions extravagantly.

'I don't quite know how to go about this,' she said. For the benefit of observers she was beaming at me lovingly.

'Try the straight approach. Spit in my face, call me Horse.'

'It's not that. Well, all right—Cliff, the word around here is that you and I are finished.'

'That's what I heard. I thought it pretty weird.'

'Weird?'

'Last time I saw you we had a mild—difference of opinion. Nothing new, I thought. But before I see you again I'm told we're finished. It didn't come from me.'

'It didn't?'

'Jesus, Julie!'

'It didn't? It really didn't?'

'Fucking hell! Listen, Julie, I just arrived in this town.'

'I know, but . . .'

'The only person I've spoken to is Rod. Honest.'

'Ah, well, Rod . . .'

'Oh, I know he fancies you. But he's my friend. He wouldn't.'

'No.'

'Why did you say we had to have this conversation before dinner?'

'Oh Cliff, that's cruel. No, all right, it's straight. Because if it went the wrong way . . .'

'I'd be looking for a bed?'

'That's about it. Sorry.'

'Jesus!'

'Sorry.'

I took a deep breath. This was horrible. I could feel my whole life coming to an edge.

'Can I tell you something?' I said urgently.

'Oh do, please! Tell me something!'

'I fell in love with you this evening. Hopelessly. Totally. Before I just loved you, you know. I did love you. But this is different. Suffering.'

Silence. Quite a long silence. Julie was deeply frowning. I began to panic.

'Julie, listen . . .'

'When?'

'When what?'

'When did you fall in love with me?'

'At the circus. When you were smiling like a fool, and clapping, and the tears were raining out of your eyes like diamonds.'

'That's pretty stupid.'

'I know.'

She flicked me a smile. 'If I believe you,' she said, 'it's only because I want to.'

'That sounds good.'

'Because, you know—that rumour—I thought maybe you'd put it about to make it easy for you to ditch me.'

'I had the same thought about you, but rejected it on the grounds of your high moral character.'

Julie sucked on her teeth and said 'Shit!' and I knew she meant it. My heart lifted.

'Someone around here must have hot pants for you. Rumours don't start themselves.'

'I guess that's it.'

'Larry Instone?'

Julie blinked at me.

'I'll kill him,' I said.

'Not necessary. I told him I wasn't available.'

'So did Rodney.'

We both glanced towards the bar, but either Instone had gone or was peering hopefully at us from hiding.

'It's all right, Cliff. Honest. It's you I'm interested in.'

'Tell me more.'

'I love you. I'm in love with you.'

'I never heard anything so good in my life. As of when?'

'It was at the Peace Camp,' said Julie, looking shifty again. 'It's pretty crazy, because when I got there I was thinking I might have to ditch you.'

'I had a notion you might be.'

'Because I'm stuck with this, you know. More than ever, after spending three nights with those wonderful women at the camp. Nothing will shift me, Cliff.'

'I never tried to. Did I? Did I?'

'No. You've been good about it. But it was annoying, the fact that I couldn't make you see it my way, when it all seems so obvious to me. Sometimes I felt it was—well, a deliberate tease. I couldn't live with that. But then, over the weekend . . .'

'You bethought you of John Keats?'

'No, you fool! Don't back off like that. Oh Christ, don't you *see*? It was *their* honesty, their absolute consistency . . . Oh fuck!'

I saw. We were holding hands, all four hands, across the table by now, and when Julie saw that I saw she grinned madly at me, and I grinned madly back. For the moment we'd nothing more to say; for the future, everything. Rodney, Selina and Walter, with a sure sense for the natural end of a scene, came now to stand in a semicircle behind us. They looked pleased with us. I had to say something light to wrap it up.

'So I'm an honorary upside down inside out Peace Camp woman, is that it?'

Julie said, 'Away, you starveling, you eel-skin, you dried neat's-tongue, you bull's pizzle, you stock-fish, you tailor's yard, you sheath, you bow-case, you vile standing hulk.'

'Wrong play,' we all said.

Doing the Voices

'My father was eaten by a lion,' Harry told Maureen, in cadences he had perfected over the years. 'Not many people can say that. And my mother missed her trapeze so often they called her Bouncing Lil. We're a family of failures, you see. Well, Dad's lion had an infected paw, you couldn't blame the lion, Dad ought to have noticed. Mum just missed her trapeze once too often—there was a hole in the net that time. She was responsible for checking the net, so she couldn't complain. Well, she didn't get a chance to, being dead.'

'And what about you, then?' asked Maureen, wide-eyed.

'Oh, I've failed at so many things it would make your foot go to sleep listening to them.'

They were sitting in the soft back seats of Harry's 1929 Rolls-Royce limousine at the far edge of the orchard, out of sight of the Hall where they both worked, Maureen as Lady Luke's maid, Harry as what Sir Henry liked to call 'my Estate Steward'. Behind them was Harry's much more modern and comfortable caravan, but Maureen wouldn't go in there. There was a bed visible through the window. Maureen was a virgin, and afraid of self-invited rape.

'Oh, go on, don't be mean. Tell me.'

Harry enjoyed giving his spiel about his parents. It was largely true, and outside the scope of most people's experience. He was aware that its recital bestowed on him a slightly raffish

99

air which, with the right audience, he quite enjoyed. He was less enthusiastic about giving his own history, not because he was ashamed of it but because it bored him, it seemed irrelevant to his present promising situation. But he was very keen on Maureen, getting keener all the time, and wanted to please her.

'Don't you think we ought to go back?'

'In a bit. We've only been ten minutes. Oh come on, Harry, *please!*'

Maureen hadn't had Harry to herself before, for this long, and in such a forthcoming mood. She wasn't going to waste her chance. Anyway, it was Christmas Eve. Everything, she felt vaguely, ought to be different on Christmas Eve.

'Well, briefly, after Mum got herself killed, I got the sack.'

'From what?'

'The circus, silly. It's all family, you know, circus is. I was a clown by then, but a very bad clown.'

'Why very bad?' Maureen felt Harry stirring restlessly beside her on the smelly leather seat and sensed his resistance to telling her more. Recklessly, dangerously, she slipped her arm through his and squeezed it against her side. Harry could, as Maureen well knew, feel her soft plump breast against his arm. What she didn't know was that this almost instantly gave him an erection. He sat close to her, very still, entranced by his sensations.

'Harry! Come on! Why very bad?'

'I don't know. No, that's not true. I do. I couldn't find a true character. I didn't know whether I was Harlequin or Pierrot. Or rather . . .'

Harry was becoming alarmed by the intensity of his desire. At the same time another alarm occurred in the shape of the qualification he was about to make.

'Or rather what?' said Maureen fiercely, squeezing his arm against her breast.

'Or rather, sometimes I felt Harlequin, and sometimes Pierrot, and I never knew which it was going to be. It upset everybody.'

'I don't know what you mean. Harlequin, Pierrot? They're just names to me. I don't follow.'

'Well, you wouldn't, would you? Why should you?' Harry, in his turn, gave Maureen's arm a significant squeeze. He said urgently, 'Mave . . . listen . . . Mave . . . !'

'What?'

Harry struggled with himself. In a strangled voice he said, 'Mave . . . Mave, let's go back!'

It might have meant, back there, into the caravan; or back to the Hall. Harry didn't know which it meant.

'Oh, Harry, *why?* We've only been . . .'

Then Maureen noticed the source of Harry's discomfort, a second before he covered it with a casually laid sleeve. She was out of the Rolls-Royce before Harry could even register embarrassment, or contrition, or importunity, or whichever cocktail of these he was feeling.

As they walked back towards the Hall, treading on rotten apples and pears, Maureen asked, 'So then what did you do?'

'Oh, we had family connections with the showmen. I got a job as a gaff-lad on the Three Abreast Horses. I was with them for quite a while. But then I fucked up again.'

'How?'

'You do ask a lot of questions, Mave.'

'Well, I'm interested.'

Harry thought about that. He couldn't quite see why. She was quite young. Bog Irish Catholic. Probably still a virgin. Not stupid, in fact very bright. Pretty. Lovely body, oh dear yes. Why should she be interested in a thirty-two year old failure: failed clown (though not for the reason given to Maureen); failed gaff-lad; failed husband (he dipped his head in acknowledgement to Christine as she drifted through his thought); failed—so far, *so* far!—composer of popular songs. He was also, he knew, an anachronism, born middle-aged into a dying culture, out of contact with his own generation in the flattie world. Maureen thought of him, he knew, as 'educated', but that was a sham. Because of his showman background he could do the voices, had learned to type, and could put one word after another. Educated he wasn't. He could fool Lady Luke—easily; he could just about fool Sir Henry; but he couldn't fool Albert, the gamekeeper, who came from Hackney and knew one when he saw one. For a flattie, Albert had more nous than he ought to have. At an early stage in their acquaintance Albert had said, 'Here, Saucebottle, I got your number! You're a stallholder, that's what you are! You're a bloody side-street spieler! Jesus! Some of us get lucky!'

Harry had disdained to engage Albert in argument; he knew when he'd been seen, so why bother? His position was only marginally endangered by Albert's percipience, and then only if Harry made an enemy of him, which was unlikely. He liked Albert, and respected him. But he was wishing, now, that he had not been so forthcoming with Maureen. You never knew with girls. Would she pass it on?

'Look, Mave,' he said awkwardly, kicking at smelly brown apples, 'keep all that stuff to yourself, will you? What I told you, parents, circus, showmen, all that? It wouldn't help me here if that got around.'

Maureen was indignant. 'You don't have to say that,' she told him. 'I'm not an eejit, I know what it's like in service. And I got my own secrets.'

'Tell me.'

Maureen stopped, became grave. They leant their shoulders, one each side, against the trunk of an ancient pear tree whose hard fruit littered the ground, too woody to rot. They looked through lichen-festooned twigs towards the jumbled outbuildings at the back of the brutal Jacobean mansion. In the yard Len could be seen chopping short logs into kindling. A Suffolk man, Len did not hurry at his work. Maureen said, 'You'll never tell? It's a straight swap, right?'

'You're safe as a sunbeam with me, Mave.'

'I'm writing a book. A novel. It's about sex.'

Harry nodded seriously, trying to see round the tree trunk to check that he wasn't being put on. He was sure he wasn't. What else would a twenty-four-year-old Catholic virgin want to write about? Maureen said in a rush, 'Oh Harry, it's terrible difficult, fighting the words, trying to tell the truth. It really hurts, you know?'

Harry didn't. He knew about words, the wretched things, because one day he was going to be a famous song writer. But he had very little experience of telling the truth.

Maureen said tentatively, 'Do you think you could help me? With the words? Grammar, punctuation, and that?'

Harry felt let down. So that was it. That was what she wanted. His supposed literacy. What a bummer.

'Have to see, won't we?' he said lightly, and strode off towards his immediate objective, a window.

Maureen watched him go sadly. Well, I blew that, she thought. Of course, she wasn't in the same class as him, she knew that, but he'd been so nice to her recently, nicer and nicer in fact, she had begun to wonder. But if it was only sex, like the rest of the men she'd encountered, well, she wasn't interested. But what a beauty, she thought longingly, what a beauty! Harry was tall, Maureen had always gone for tall men, with a mop of black curly hair and the sort of creamy, transparent skin that always made him look as if he needed another shave half way through the day. In the summer she had seen him working with Len, laying land-drains they were, under the drive where the puddle always was, and Harry had his shirt off and she had marvelled at his lovely skin and muscles like an athlete's. How come he wasn't married, a man like that? It was wicked, it was a waste. But she couldn't see him lasting in this boring old place, he was too good for it, he'd just up and go one day, and she'd be left. Snuffling a bit, not miserable, just sad, she went off to find out whether she'd been missed.

Lady Luke couldn't find any of her staff. She knew that Hans and Gerda were in the kitchen, preparing titbits for Sir Henry's Christmas Eve staff party, and that Mrs Pantry could be relied upon to come through with a decent lunch for Sir Henry and herself once the party was over, but these weren't the people she wanted. Where was Len and the kindling for the hall fire? Where was Harry? Where was Albert, who was supposed to perform, parallel to his gamekeeping duties, certain essential domestic chores? And above all, where was Maureen? Lady Luke had unsuccessfully rung for her several times before penetrating the hostile territory between her drawing-room and the kitchen in search of her. Oh yes, Hans assured her in his enthusiastic teutonic tones, Maureen had passed through the kitchen only a few minutes before, delivering newly ironed sheets to the downstairs airing cupboard, but he couldn't say where she was now. And Mister Harry, well, he thought Mister Harry was in the Estate Office.

Lady Luke had to pass the door of the Estate Office on her way back from the kitchen, along the bleak corridor that led to the vast, icy, oak-panelled hall where Sir Henry's staff party would be held. She paused outside the office to listen for the sound of Harry's typewriter, or perhaps for a snatch of strange song, for Harry often sung his own compositions while he worked. She could hear nothing, and she didn't knock. It was the only room in the Hall which Sir Henry had specifically forbidden her to enter, on the grounds that he had not married her for her business abilities and had no wish for conversation related to the running of the estate. This, though true, was not his main reason for the ban. Sir Henry kept his collection of soft pornography at the back of one of the filing cabinet drawers. The cabinet was locked, but Sir Henry had a delicate distaste for the thought of his collection and his wife being in the same room.

Safely back in her drawing-room, Lady Luke moved about aimlessly, plumping pillows that had already been plumped, adjusting the angles of family photographs that had already been adjusted, and wondering if she should make a list, and if so, a list of what? There were so many things that had to be done, she was sure, but for the moment she couldn't think what those things were. The fact that Sir Henry had not yet rung to tell her what time he would be arriving back from London paralysed her will. She rang the bell again and, when Maureen failed to appear, went back out into the freezing hall to see whether it would remind her of what she had to do. A thin, pretty woman, usually vivacious, she looked now haggard with worry, middle-aged at thirty-five.

Isobel, in a dressing gown, tousle-haired and blowsy with sleep, was slowly descending the grand flight of stairs that led directly into the hall and guaranteed its winter iciness. Isobel was Sir Henry's niece and, to his grave disappointment, his only heir apart from his wife, marriage to whom was his third attempt to establish a male line of inheritance for the fortune he had built and the 'family seat' he had acquired to honour it. Isobel had been a weekend hippie in the 'Sixties. Now nearly as old as her step-aunt, she was trying to be a successful businesswoman, running an expensive print gallery near Sloane Square, but her heart wasn't in it. She still craved excitement, freedom, romance.

'Morning,' she said, yawning.

'Oh, there you are at last!' cried Lady Luke, relieved at the sight of an unthreatening face. 'It's almost ten, you know.'

'So what? It's Christmas Eve, there's nothing needs doing, not by me anyway. I only came down because I was bored with my own company.'

'The house seems to be completely dead,' Lady Luke told her. 'I can't find a soul.'

'Who do you want, and what for?' Isobel was lighting a cigarette. Her step-aunt, who had recently given them up, managed to refrain from complaining. 'Well, for a start,' she said, 'I want somebody to go along to the greenhouses and ask Pantry for some flowers.'

Pantry, the nurseryman, who at Sir Henry's urging unsuccessfully attempted to run the nursery garden as a profit-making commercial enterprise, was at this moment approaching along the service corridor with an armful of flowers. Lady Luke was incorrectly supposed, by Sir Henry, to enjoy flower-arranging; and Pantry, although he always claimed that the production of flowers for Christmas was a waste of good greenhouse space, knew his duty. Reaching the green baize door he opened it a fraction with his foot. Lady Luke's plaintive voice drifted through to him, thinned by the vast spaces of the hall and stairwell.

'. . . darling, I know it's ridiculous, but whenever I want to ask Pantry for something I get all sweaty and nervous, and in the end I always have to ask someone else to do it. He's such an *angry* little man.'

'Well, I'm not going,' said Isobel with finality. 'He gives me the creeps. If you like I'll go and ask Harry . . .'

Pantry let the service door close silently and made his way, with his armful of flowers, back down the long cold corridor. On the way he encountered Len, bearing bundles of faggots neatly secured with strips of willow-bark. Len was a country craftsman, and proud of it.

'Herself's in the hall,' said Pantry.

Without a word Len turned about and followed Pantry out to the yard. They passed Albert, coming in. 'Happy Christmas, chummies,' said Albert, but got no reply.

'Thank you, darling,' said Lady Luke to Isobel. 'But do get dressed first, and, *please*, darling, not jeans—you know Henry likes to see us girls in a skirt.'

'I do know, I do know,' said Isobel lightly, thinking, I do know he's a dirty old man.

Albert knocked on the door of the Estate Office, listened for a moment, then opened the door a crack. The little room was empty save for its grey steel filing cabinets, and the desk with its wire baskets and electric typewriter, but Albert waited, knowing what he knew. After a few moments the decorative wrought-iron handle of the casement window started to move downwards, as if of its own volition. Albert couldn't see it, but he was aware of the thin, strong wire which was attached to the spiral handle and which ran down the central iron divider and out under the window's lower edge. Free of its catch, the window opened outwards. Fingertips appeared. Albert narrowed the crack between door and jamb. A foot threw itself across the sill of the window, its heel finding purchase enough to lever forward until a whole foreleg and knee were in sight. Albert closed the door softly and waited. He waited patiently, glancing up and down the corridor occasionally, until he heard the ratchet of Harry's typewriter roller winding a sheet of paper into the machine. He knocked.

'Come!' Harry had learned that from Sir Henry, and relished it. Albert entered the Estate Office.

'Ah, there you are,' said Harry unaccusingly. 'I thought the whole place was asleep. You've brought the egg returns?'

'Not so much asleep,' said Albert, 'as grazing. We all got our own patches to graze, don't we?'

'Don't know about you,' said Harry, 'but I've got my bloody weekly report to finish, so . . . you wanted something?'

'No.'

'You brought the egg returns?'

'No.'

'So what the fuck are you doing in here?'

'Looking at you,' said Albert, 'wiv a mixture of admiration and sorrow.'

'Albert, come on. In a couple of hours Sir Henry'll be back and he'll want . . .'

'You don't know the half of what he'll want,' Albert said, 'but I'm here to tell you. If you can afford half an hour dallying with Maureen in the orchard you can afford five minutes of valuable advice from Albert.'

Harry looked at Albert cautiously. 'Now, Albert, you know perfectly well I've been slaving away in here for . . .'

'Come off it, Saucebottle,' said Albert impatiently.

'Saucebottle' dated from Albert's discovery, while nosing about, as he liked to do, through his employer's private papers, of Harry's reply to Sir Henry's advertisement in the Personal Column of *The Times*. Sir Henry had advertised: 'All round handyman/chauffeur required for country estate in Essex. Rolls-Royce experience an asset.' Harry, whose parents had christened him Henry Peter, had replied, enclosing copious references, including an excellent one from his ex-wife and ex-employer Christine, signing his letter 'H. P. Saunderson'. Albert's initially crude 'HP Sauce' had evolved into 'Sauce-bottle'. Harry, feeling it on the whole an affectionate soubriquet, made no objection.

To Harry's enquiring silence Albert said, 'I saw you come frough vat window minutes ago. I saw you sweet-talking Maureen in the orchard. You want jam on it? Don't waste my time.'

Harry nodded his head busily, looking utterly satisfied with what he was hearing. He beamed at Albert. 'Tell me the good news,' he said.

'It's about Sir Henry's little party,' said Albert, pleased with Harry's response. 'For the one, everybody needs to know what time it's on. That's down to you to find out and spread around. For the other, you got to know that after we drink the loyal toast . . .'

'Loyal toast, Albert?'

'Abso-bloody-lutely. What it's about, Saucebottle, what it's about. And that's where you come in.'

Harry said nothing, just widened his eyes. He didn't for a moment think that Albert was kidding him, but did begin to wonder what he'd got into.

'You got to lead the singing,' said Albert, a note of pity in his voice.

'I see. What's the song, Albert?'

'Freeza jolly good fellow.'

'I see.'

They looked at each other with mutual sympathy, the cockney gamekeeper and the travelling man, united in astonishment at the world they inhabited.

'I'll tip you the wink, see, when the moment comes. Don't be shy. We'll all follow.'

'Who proposes the loyal toast?'

'Pantry, of course.'

Harry's face split into a delighted grin. 'Of course, of course! If anyone round here hates Sir Henry's guts, it's Pantry.'

'You got it, mate,' said Albert, thinking, I can live with this weird geezer.

'Thanks, Albert. I'm glad you told me.'

'Thought you'd like to know, Saucebottle,' said Albert cheerfully. 'We wouldn't want to spoil Sir Henry's party, would we?'

'Damn right we wouldn't,' said Harry with determination. 'Egg returns.'

'Later,' said Albert, drifting away. 'Don't forget, time of party. Some 'as got families.'

'I'll go now,' said Harry.

When Harry knocked on the door of Lady Luke's drawing-room she called 'Come!' Harry resolved not to use this response again. Lady Luke was sitting sideways on the upholstered stool before her escritoire. She was wearing a short tight skirt which displayed her handsome knees shining through nylon so fine that Harry suspected she was wearing stockings rather than tights, a thesis supported by evidence from elsewhere. She was making a list.

'Ah, Harry, good. Do you know where Maureen is? I've rung and rung.'

'Ironing sheets when I last saw her, Lady Luke.'

Lady Luke frowned. She didn't like being called 'Lady Luke' by Harry. Her own education had gone no higher than secretarial college, and she wouldn't be surprised to find that Harry had a university degree, though not, she thought, from Oxford or Cambridge. But one couldn't tell these days. Since no blandishments of hers would make Harry talk about himself this remained only a suspicion, but it was enough to make her uncomfortable in his presence.

'You might ask her to come and see me, if you run into her. I've got so much to do, and no help at all. In fact I wondered—I was just wondering—if perhaps you couldn't help me wrap the presents for the staff . . . ?'

Sometimes Lady Luke asked Harry to sit down, which he usually declined to do. Now he decided to sit down without being asked, but to make it something less than a challenge he compromised by perching on the arm of a leather-covered chair.

'I'm afraid I'm very busy, Lady Luke, trying to finish the weekly report for Sir Henry, you know how keen he is on the weekly report.'

'I do,' said Lady Luke bitterly. It was yet another of those areas of Sir Henry's life to which she had no access. Suddenly it all seemed too much, she felt like crying, she desperately needed some personal support.

'Harry,' she pleaded, 'for Christ's sake, couldn't you drop the Lady Luke stuff when we're alone? I know what you are, you know what I am. I feel so *alone* here!'

Harry's heart melted a little, but not enough. Her choice of words was unfortunate. He didn't like to be told so confidently by this silly woman that she knew what he was when she was patently stuck miles up a gum tree.

'I don't think Sir Henry would like it if I called you Celia, Lady Luke,' he told her.

'For God's sake Harry, Henry isn't *here!*'

'No. But it would be very difficult for me to switch backwards and forwards. And in front of Albert, or Maureen . . . no, it's easier for me this way. Really, I'd have thought it would be easier for you.'

'Well, fuck you,' said Lady Luke. She turned back to her escritoire.

'About the party,' said Harry, standing, carefully keeping his voice at the same matter-of-fact level, 'everybody wants to know . . .'

'I know they do. I know they do. So do I. But he hasn't phoned yet. As soon as he phones . . .' She crossed something off her list with a savage jab of her gold biro, as if, thought Harry, she was crossing his name off a guest list.

'Yes, Lady Luke. Just one other thing. I did wonder whether I ought to mention, in my weekly report, the Land-Rover's broken half-shaft?'

Lady Luke swivelled on her stool, her eyes narrow. 'Harry,' she said very quietly, 'if you know what's good for you, what's *good* for you, Harry, you will not now or *ever* mention the Land-Rover's broken half-shaft. Do you understand?'

'Oh yes, Lady Luke,' said Harry happily. He wished he felt free to do a back-flip and walk out of the room on his hands. Instead he bowed, which was a bit feeble since Lady Luke had her back to him again.

Maureen and Bobby, the 'outside boy', knowing without the help of Lady Luke's lists what had to be done, were hanging up paperchains in the hall. They had two pairs of step ladders, a pile of chains on the floor, and a roll of fawn masking tape each. Harry watched them from the darkness of the stone archway that led to Lady Luke's drawing-room. Maureen, up her ladder, was stretching up to fix one end of the chain to the heavy gilded frame of a dark portrait—somebody's ancestor, but not Sir Henry's. Harry could see a pretty line of lace where the hem of Maureen's petticoat showed. Bobby must have an even better view. Bobby, on the bottom of his own ladder, held the other end of the paper chain.

'For the love of God,' Maureen cried, 'don't go pulling on the things all the time! They're not made of elastic.'

'It won't reach, Mave.'

'It'll reach if you move your ladder nearer, you poor eejit. And don't call me Mave, I don't like it.'

'Harry does.'

'*Mister* Harry to you, Bobby. And Mister Harry can do what he likes. He's entitled.'

Bobby chuckled lewdly, moving his ladder so as to get a better view up Maureen's skirt. 'Oh yeah? Do what he likes, can he?'

Harry was about to break this nonsense up by showing himself when he noticed that the service door was opening. He waited. Hans, carrying a tray of glasses, appeared. He turned and held the door open with his foot while Gerda came through with a tray of savoury snacks. Hans followed Gerda across the hall to the long oak refectory table beyond which Maureen and Bobby were working.

'Ooh, look!' cried Maureen. 'Lovely tasty little things! Well done, Gerda.'

'There is more to carry,' said Gerda, at rather than to Hans. He ignored her.

'Tell him there is more food to carry,' Gerda said to Maureen.

'Gerda says . . .'

'Tell her glasses is my work, food is her work,' Hans said to Maureen.

'Hans says . . .'

'Tell him glasses is not work, is play,' said Gerda, busily unloading dishes from her tray and arranging them on the table. 'Tell him I have only two hands and he, pig, will eat the food.'

'She says . . .' said Bobby and Maureen together.

'Tell her, she, sow, will drink from glasses,' said Hans. 'Tell her, my Gott in heaven, she make my life purgatorical.'

'Tell him,' snapped Gerda triumphantly, not waiting for the message to be relayed, 'in English the noun "purgatory" makes the adjective "purgatorial", and is uncommon.'

Harry came out into the body of the hall. 'That'll do you two,' he said. 'And you'd better not carry on like that in front of Sir Henry and Lady Luke when you come to the staff party. Go back to the kitchen and make it up.'

'Yes, sir, Mister Harry, sir,' said Hans. He and Gerda grabbed their trays and scuttled away. Harry knew that both of them regarded him as all-knowing and all-powerful, a far more potent authority figure than either Sir Henry or Lady Luke. He had decided that this was because he was, unlike Lady Luke, always ready to make a positive decision, where arguable choices existed, no matter what department of the hall's affairs might be affected. His decisions, being arbitrary, came quickly and with confidence, thus relieving others of the burden of worrying about whether they were the correct decisions or not. Albert merely enjoyed this knack of Harry's. To Hans and Gerda it was awesome.

'Her ladyship longs for your company,' he told Maureen. 'Just a sec'.'

'Bobby could do that himself, you know. He's only stupid when you're around.'

This truth, known to them all, brought Maureen down from her ladder smiling. Harry suddenly felt irrationally happy. He felt the spirit move in him and couldn't resist it. He went down on his hands, threw his feet in the air, and walked the whole length of the hall on his hands. At the service door he paused, gave it a kick, and disappeared through the open door, upside down. The door swung closed.

'Did you see that?' said Bobby, as if he couldn't believe what he'd seen. 'Jesus, I could never do that!'

'Begob,' said Maureen, 'no more could I!'

Bobby eyed her, wishing she would.

Although one of the filing cabinets in the Estate Office was kept locked, the key remaining in Sir Henry's possession, locks were no problem to Harry. Isobel sat on the edge of Harry's desk reading an example from Sir Henry's collection. Harry tapped slowly at his typewriter with two fingers.

'Listen to this, Harry,' said Isobel. ' "Claudia realised that Nigel's hand had somehow moved from her knee"—I like that "somehow", somehow—"and up her nylon-clad thigh to come to a momentary rest only a fraction of an inch below the top of her stocking. How had this happened? Somehow"—there it is again—"Somehow in the deep swoon of his kisses"—hey, dig that deep swoon—"she had not noticed. Now she could not but notice as his light touch ventured beyond the nylon to stroke naked, tingling flesh. Claudia's whole body felt as if charged with vibrant electricity." Does that turn you on, Harry?'

'No. I don't belong to the stocking-top generation. But there's stuff in that cabinet that does. I rather resent it.'

'I know. So do I.'

This ambiguity brought Harry to look at her. What was she resenting, his response to some of Sir Henry's mildly dirty books, or her own? He regarded Isobel as a dangerous woman, largely because he could not easily read the overtones and undertones of her classless voice and dated slang, but he appreciated her frank, open sexuality. He hadn't seen her wearing a skirt before; the garment became her. Her legs were a pleasure to regard. He typed a full stop, carefully, and regarded them. Isobel went on reading.

Maureen knocked on the door and, without waiting for a response, entered. Harry dragged his eyes away from Isobel's legs a moment too late.

'Flowers,' Maureen said.

'I know,' said Isobel easily, 'that what I'm here for too. I've asked him. He said he would.'

Harry stood up and came out from behind his desk. He could sense an atmosphere, and didn't like it. Between them these two women had contrived to make him feel guilty, although he knew he had wronged neither. He slipped the book from Isobel's fingers, dropped it into the back of the open filing drawer, closed the drawer and locked the cabinet. It was done with such despatch that Isobel was left looking at her empty fingers in disbelief. She didn't know where she was with this one.

'Okay, Mave,' said Harry. 'For you I'll do it.'

Maureen backed out, smiling. Isobel looked at the closed

door. 'You shouldn't encourage her,' she said. 'She's a brazen wench.'

'That's how I like wenches,' said Harry. 'Brazen. And now the flowers.'

Harry went to seek out Pantry in his hot and smelly greenhouses. The nursery was in a hollow, a bank surrounding it on three sides, perhaps the relic of a moat or some other defensive earthwork; for the Hall, though in its present form undistinguished, was of ancient lineage, the family that had yielded to Sir Henry's cash offer boasting pre-Conquest nobility in these parts. Pantry's cottage, where Mrs Pantry, when not cooking for Lady Luke, wrestled with the whims of three aggressive children, lay below the eastern bank, the two greenhouses nestling nearby. These three buildings, and some other small wooden structures, were all connected by a network of covered duckboards so that Pantry would not get his bald head wet, nor his shoes muddy, while going about his business. He had spent much of his own time, and of Sir Henry's money, on these arrangements, which he insisted were 'economically essential', an argument that always won favour with Sir Henry if surrounded by enough arcane detail.

Harry entered the greenhouse nearest the Hall's yard by its double-glazed door. Heat and humidity embraced him, and the threatening exhalations of vegetable growth. There were no flowers in here: lettuces, most of them run to seed, sweet peppers, bush tomatoes, blackfly-encrusted broad beans, defied the bitter winter. 'I haven't got six hands, have I?' Pantry was fond of saying. That the nursery was understaffed was obvious.

In the second greenhouse, the one nearer to the cottage, there was more order. Here flowers predominated. Although Pantry claimed to despise flowers they appeared to be well looked after. This was where Harry found him, plunging the cut ends of chrysanthemum stalks into boiling water.

'I've got more of these than she'll want,' he told Harry. 'But you can't sell 'em. There's no market for 'em. So what does he expect, I ask you? What does he expect?'

An uneasy truce existed between Harry and Pantry, both knowing that war could very easily break out but that it would be to neither's advantage. They kept their distance, remaining uninquisitive about each other's affairs. An as yet uncharted minefield lay in the complex question of staff precedence. Mrs Pantry was known to have strong feelings on the subject.

'You can take these,' said Pantry, thrusting into Harry's arms the bundle of chrysanthemums he had very nearly delivered to the Hall himself. Harry looked meaningfully at the fresher, more showy flowers whose stems Pantry had been treating in order to prolong the life of the blooms. He knew that Pantry must have a market for these or he wouldn't have cut and treated them, but reserved the knowledge for possible future use. Pantry saw the look and interpreted it correctly. 'You written your report for Sir Henry?' he said truculently.

'I have,' said Harry, knowing what was coming.

'You told him about my elm?'

'I have.'

'That man round Thursday. He a timber merchant?'

'He was.'

'What he say?'

'The tree's dying. He'll pay twenty pounds for the timber if he can take it out next week. If he can't have it next week he's not interested.'

Pantry nodded heavily. The dying elm, which leaned over his cottage in a threatening way, had been his main, almost his only, topic of conversation with Harry for the past six months.

'So you told him to go ahead?'

'Subject to Sir Henry's approval.'

Pantry moved off down the greenhouse, muttering. Harry couldn't hear what he was saying, but knew the substance of it: has to ask Sir Henry before he wipes his bottom. Harry had

heard it before. Festooned with blooms, he returned to the hall.
Fuck Pantry, he thought. It was all in the weekly report.

Harry dumped the armful of wilting chrysanthemums on the
Estate Office desk. Isobel was still there. Harry noted that he
was pleased about this. She was sitting in his chair, leafing
through the contents of the basket marked FILE. Its main
interest for her appeared to be the carbon copies of past Weekly
Reports. Harry perched himself on the edge of the desk beside
the flowers and once again admired Isobel's crossed legs. The
faint down of hair that was apparent on either side of her
kneecaps was particularly attractive to him; that would have
been spoiled by tights or stockings.

'Find anything interesting?' he enquired.

Isobel was thoughtful. She had a whole pile of reports,
perhaps covering three months, in one hand, and she slapped at
them irritably with the other.

'I don't like these,' she said. 'Okay, so you had some holes in
the drive filled and it cost so much, you had Len thin out a
coppice because Albert said the birds couldn't get up through
it, Bobby's cleaning the first floor windows but you'll have to
buy a longer ladder if he's to get at the second floor, the
Land-Rover's mysteriously out of action, the egg returns are
down because of the cold weather and may you please buy some
heavy duty tyres for the mini-tractor . . .'

'That's what my job is,' said Harry, interrupting her.
'Dealing with trivia.'

'I don't object to that,' said Isobel. 'But that's the *only*
substance in these reports. The rest is fiction.'

'Yes,' said Harry. Good God, he thought, here's a sharp little
flattie, she'd run a good rig.

'You know what I mean?' Isobel insisted. 'Stuff about
thatches you've never even looked at, stuff about village
festivals that never happened, stuff about local characters who
don't even fucking *exist*!'

'Yes,' said Harry patiently. 'But, you know, most of the time nothing happens here, there's nothing to report. And Sir Henry has to have his weekly report, he wouldn't feel safe without it. So I make things up. What's wrong with that?'

'And he doesn't see?'

Harry took his eyes away from Isobel's knees and attended to her face. She was a puzzle. He had her down as a me-first person, but suddenly he realised she was worrying not about herself, nor about Harry, but about her Uncle Henry. That didn't fit with the Sloane Square image he had assigned to her. Not that Harry had ever been to Sloane Square—Hampstead Heath Fair was the furthest he had penetrated into London—but he thought he knew, from casual perusal of Lady Luke's glossy magazines, the style and ethos that would prevail in the area where Isobel had her gallery. It didn't mesh with this sort of concern.

He said carefully, 'Sir Henry is obviously a brilliant businessman. But as far as this place is concerned, he's a romantic. I try to feed that. That's all.'

'You're doing a bloody good job of it,' said Isobel. 'It makes a pretty picture. But I can't see how he buys it.'

'He buys it,' said Harry. Isobel's challenging look changed suddenly to one of perplexity. Harry went on guard.

'You're a strange creature,' Isobel said, exactly as Harry had expected. 'I can't place you at all. Where are you from?'

'Wales,' said Harry. It was his stock response to this sort of probe. He'd travelled on the Welsh circuit once, after Christine had sacked him, and had realised that this nation embraced many different types of people.

'That figures,' said Isobel. 'The Welsh don't seem to have much of a class system, do they? You haven't got a Welsh accent, though.'

'I've travelled a lot,' said Harry.

'Why? And where? Tell me.'

Here we go, thought Harry. Another of 'em. Why couldn't they just take him as he presented himself?

'Would you mind, Miss Luke,' he said, 'if I took the liberty of calling you Miss Isobel?'

'You are a shit,' said Isobel. It seemed to hang in the balance for an instant, but then she laughed, a good guffaw of genuine amusement. Harry liked that.

'You call me Isobel or nothing,' she said, still smiling.

'I can handle Isobel okay,' said Harry. He hadn't used her name before. But nor had he ever called her Miss Luke.

'Do you suppose you'll hold this job for long?' Isobel asked.

'As long as Sir Henry will have me.'

'That's no answer.'

'It's the only one I've got.'

'I don't believe it. There's more to you than being Uncle Henry's gun dog.'

'Nice of you to say so,' said Harry.

Isobel got up from behind the desk, allowing the pile of weekly reports on her lap to slide to the floor. Okay, thought Harry, tit for tat, fair enough. She came round the desk and stood close to him.

'Do you find me attractive?' she asked.

'Very,' said Harry.

'Good,' said Isobel. She gathered up the armful of flowers from the desk top and looked at Harry across the blooms, smiling. 'So hang around, right?' Harry found no answer to this. When Isobel had left the room he looked at his hands. The palms were sweaty. Yes, he did find her attractive. And yes, he knew of her financial prospects, and found those attractive too. But how long can a man keep on doing the voices?

His weekly report finished, Harry wondered how to occupy the next couple of hours or more before Sir Henry's party. He could do himself some good with Celia by issuing forth and offering to wrap presents, but wasn't too concerned about doing himself good in that direction and anyway felt vaguely that such activity would impair his dignity, or his status, or both.

He could sneak back to the Rolls and have a look at the song he was currently writing. He had turned the spacious rear-compartment of the limousine into an office, the tip-up seats behind the partition providing the bases for, on the left, a desk that held his thirty-five year old typewriter, and, on the right, an angled board for his sheet music and a rest for his clarinet. It was all very comfortable and convenient, and Harry was never so happy as when lying back in the deeply upholstered rear seats and regarding his creative arrangements. He spent hours there, every working day, confident that if there were anyone actively seeking him in the Hall Maureen would find occasion to hang a white cloth out of her bedroom window, which he could just see above the top branches of the fruit trees.

But on this Christmas Eve Harry felt he ought to keep in touch with any interesting events the Hall itself might yield. He was wondering whether to go and look for Mauren when she opened the office door, again without knocking. He'd have to speak to her about that, Harry determined, thinking of Isobel's legs.

'Himself phoned,' Maureen announced. 'Party's half an hour late—twelve thirty. Everyone's grouching, her ladypip most of all.'

'Anything still need doing?'

''Course not,' said Maureen scornfully. 'By the time she came out with her list it was all done. Fire's going nicely, decorations up, food ready, presents wrapped—she looked a right eejit.'

'She often does,' said Harry. 'So you've got some time?'

'Well, a bit, maybe,' said Maureen cautiously. After her experience in the back of the Rolls earlier she regarded being alone with Harry as a high risk situation. Still, he was a love, he really was. She couldn't deny the slight breathlessness she experienced whenever she knew she was about to see him. And she was far from displeased to know that she could arouse in him, well, certain feelings. Not much, she assured herself, could happen in the Estate Office.

Harry, still feeling distinctly Harlequinish, needed to release more of his bottled expertise, and Maureen had now become a possible audience. 'Come in and shut the door,' he said. 'Have you got a quid? A note, I mean?'

'I might have,' said Maureen, puzzled. Was he going to borrow money? That would be a turn up. She delved into the moneybelt behind her white apron. She didn't believe in bags or purses. If they want to take my money, they'll have to take me too, she told herself, aware of the sexual overtones, and the fear. She produced a pound note.

'Okay,' said Harry. 'Put it there, on the desk. This is let's pretend. Let's pretend you've just paid for a ride on the dodgems. That's two bob, okay? So you want eighteen bob back.'

'90p,' said Maureen, nodding.

'If you like.' Although decimalisation had noticeably increased their takings, showmen were conservative about language. They went on dealing in bobs and tanners, and stuck to bobs when the tanners were taken away. Harry still had difficulty in thinking in tens, twenties, fifties, but didn't want to confuse Maureen. From the desk of his drawer he produced a handful of five and ten pence pieces.

'Right,' he said, 'you've give me a quid. So I 'op across ver floor frough ver dodgems to ver boof, where ve old lady takes your oncer off of me and gives me eighteen bob, sorry, 90p change. You wiv me?'

In Harry's mind's eye the old lady in the booth was neither old nor a lady but Christine in the pride and prime of her youth, owner of three rigs and seven stalls, the best legs on the circuit and a bosom that other gaff lads eyed with envy. Harry wasn't a tit man himself. He acknowledged the perfection of Christine's, but it was the legs that held him spellbound.

'So there's this geezer,' said Harry, 'in anovver dodgem, finks he's going to get off wiv you if he jolts you up hard enough. Bang-bang-jolt. I come skipping back wiv your change and light up on the skirt of your car. Amazing how I keep my balance, you fink, special when vis geezer jolts you right up ver backside while I'm counting change. You ready then? Hold out your hand.'

Maureen held out her hand, bewildered by the change in Harry's voice, by his perky animation, his speed.

'Now,' said Harry. '10p for the ride, right?'

'Right,' said Maureen, trying to concentrate.

'So that's ten, and now here's twenty, thirty, forty, fifty . . .' Harry counted the coins not into Maureen's hand but into the palm of his own left hand, making a pile. 'Sixty, seventy, seventy-five, eighty, eighty-five, ninety, ninety-five and five makes a hundred, okay?'

'Okay,' said Maureen.

'So you've got it, lady.' Harry tipped the pile of coins from his hand into Maureen's. She closed her fist round them. Harry did a lithe sideways skip, as if dismounting from the skirt of the dodgem. 'Vat dirty old geezer just bashed you up ver back again. You oughta get away from vat one, 'e's nasty.'

'I don't get it, Harry,' said Maureen, lost.

'Count yer change, darling,' said Harry. Maureen counted. 'Here,' she said indignantly, 'I only got 60p here.'

'Damn right you have,' said Harry, displaying the thirty pence he had trapped in the palm of his hand while tipping the coins into Maureen's. 'You been tapped, darling.'

Maureen was sufficiently familiar with male forms of boasting to know how to respond. But on this occasion she was genuinely surprised and delighted. 'Here!' she cried. 'That's clever! That's really clever!'

'It's called tapping,' said Harry modestly. 'You learn that, when you're a gaff-lad. You have to.'

Maureen was still wide-eyed with admiration when Albert knocked discreetly at the door and entered quickly.

'Yeah, Maureen,' he said, 'she's looking for you, girl. Got a new list. You better keep out of sight.' Albert looked from one to the other of them, grinning. 'Funny. I fought some'ow I might find you two in 'ere.'

He was about to go. Maureen giggled and said, 'Oh, Albert, listen! I've just been tapped!'

'You been what?' said Albert in a shocked voice. He looked at the pound note on the table, at the coins in Maureen's hand, and closed the door firmly behind him. Maureen clapped a hand across her mouth as she realised what she'd done. She looked at Harry appealingly.

'Never mind, Mave,' he said, 'great writers have to tell the truth.'

Maureen closed her eyes in agony but Albert wasn't going to be distracted from his purpose by meaningless banter. 'Come on, Saucebottle,' he said. 'Give. What's tapped?'

'I been teaching Maureen to play wiv change.' Albert nodded heavily, noticing the change in voice, fitting it all together. Harry didn't care, it was such a relief. He'd have to trust Albert anyway.

'I knew you was a spieler,' said Albert. 'Let's hear it then.'

'Not here,' said Maureen quickly.

'No, good girl, not here.' Albert thought for a moment. 'Down the old apple-pressing room, right?' It was a brilliant idea. 'We go down separate,' said Albert.

When Harry's father had been eaten by a lion, and his mother, not long afterwards, fell through a hole in her safety net (both stories nearly enough true to be worth sticking with) Harry didn't get the sack. He was, in fact, quite a good clown, despite his own feelings of ambiguity; popular with the children, who enjoyed his Harlequinish acrobatic pratfalls, and with the adults who appreciated his Pierrot-like understanding of the world's unfairness. Harry left the circus because he couldn't stand the viciousness of the dwarfs, with whom he had to share a dressing-room. They had always upset him, and he complained about them to his parents. 'Oh, they're always like that,' Mum had said sunnily. 'It's because *inside*, you know, they're big and strong. They got to show they're not afraid of anything or anybody.' Harry thought that too kind. He reckoned they were vicious because they resented their condition, and the loathsome public's enjoyment of it, and needed to take their resentment out on whatever target offered itself, sometimes on each other, more often on Harry. Harry felt he was turning into a nasty person, someone he didn't like, in self-defence. Family loyalty, and fear of the world outside the circus, kept him with the show while his parents were alive. Their deaths freed him. His inheritance, on which at the time he placed little value, was the 1929 Rolls-Royce limousine, and the caravan, and £3000 which, unexpectedly, his father had stashed away in the Post Office. Harry's discovery of this money was, he thought, the great event; it would change his life. But it was the equipage which finally changed it.

Harry's father had bought the Rolls at an auction in Queensferry in 1955. He had intended to buy a powerful van, bid for the Rolls on the whim of the moment, and got it for £40. Vintage cars had not yet established themselves as an investment, except perhaps in the minds of enthusiasts, none of whom, fortunately for Harry's family, attended that particular auction. The car was in almost perfect condition and Harry's father, a man of many skills, made it as new. Petrol, in those days, was so inexpensive that consumption was not a consideration when measured against power and reliability. The Rolls's gigantic six-cylinder engine had both. Harry grew up with the car, it was part of the family, something he never thought about except as an element contributing to the many jobs that always needed doing: polishing, painting, greasing, de-rusting, varnishing . . . He treated the Rolls as he treated the caravan, as a flattie would treat the roof over his head, a standard ingredient of life which simply needed to be kept in good nick. It was home. Indeed, in his boyhood and early youth the rear compartment of the limousine had been his bedroom, more spacious and comfortable than anything available to him in the caravan. When, in the 1970s, someone told Harry that the Rolls was probably now worth £35,000 he laughed disbelievingly. He now knew that, in its still virtually new condition, it could be sold for more than this, but he continued, if not to disbelieve it, to disregard it. He couldn't imagine life without the Rolls.

After wandering about the north of England for a few years, feeling a bit lost without the circus, doing odd jobs, collecting references, learning new skills, Harry's family connections finally brought him to the showmen, to the Fair, to Christine. He followed an advertisement in *World's Fair* to Nottingham, and there Christine hired him as a gaff-lad and, not long afterward, married him. This was not really approved of among the showmen. Christine was one of them, but Harry, for all his circus background, was not. Gaff-lads are casual labourers, however much their lives and the Fairs might intertwine. If you didn't own a rig, or at the very least a stall, you weren't a showman.

Christine put Harry, after their marriage, to managing a rig, which Harry did competently enough, and overseeing some of the stalls. Among these was a striptease stall run by a genius of a spieler who could have talked the flatties in to gaze at a bunch of carrots. It wasn't so much Harry's admiration for the stripper's legs that upset Christine—the girl could, and would, be changed—as his criticism of the spieler. 'It embarrasses me,' Harry told her. 'He promises so much and we deliver so little . . .' Christine told him that it was none of his business, that she was lucky to have the best spieler in the world and if Harry didn't like it he could lump it. They had a row, made it up, and went to bed, which was always satisfactory.

But the row had been heard. Heads nodded and tongues wagged. The showmen knew their instinct about Harry was right. They could appreciate that Christine had, in a way, got lucky. Her young man was strong, faster than most at the fitting-up, a good worker and honest with it. He did all her accounts for her, looked after the bookings, typed letters to the Guild. Very handy, but that didn't make him a showman. His values were different, they could sense it. It all came to a head over the matter of tapping.

Harry wasn't against tapping. If the flatties had an ounce of sense they'd count their change and get their money back from the booth. It would never be refused. He knew, having been one, that gaff-lads couldn't make ends meet without this contribution to their wages. What he objected to was the screw put on the gaff-lads by some of the gaffers to increase their tap so that wages could be held steady. Not all the showmen did it, he acknowledged; some actively discouraged tapping as bad for trade, some even disapproved of it on ethical grounds. Christine was not among these. She openly told her gaff-lads there'd be no work from her, next year, unless they stayed on at the same wage, and no complaints. If they needed a rise they could up the tap. Harry objected. He was, after all, her husband. His view ought at least to be listened to.

'If that's how you feel,' Christine had told him, regretfully but firmly, 'you can bugger off.' So he had. There had been no divorce. Travelling people don't believe in it. One day they might meet up again, and be pleased to discover themselves still husband and wife. You never knew.

So then he joined the Welsh circuit, back to being a gaff-lad, though occasionally promoted to managing a stall, or even a rig, when the owners had their hands full. After some quite pleasant gaffs, and some truly joyous travelling, he'd encountered a bunch of gypsies in Blaenau Ffestiniog who had offered to cut his balls off if he didn't disappear—perhaps he had admired the legs of one of their girls too openly—so Harry had motored slowly back to England, in no hurry, not at all interested in proving points. Fuck gypsies. They were always bad news. He had a nice summer, creeping gently about the Midlands, collecting a wonderful reference from a brigadier who also happened to be a lord, for whom Harry had restored the roof of an ancient barn. He ended up at Banbury Fair, looking for old friends and news of Christine. He found both. Christine had 'married' again, this time to a showman with two rigs of his own. Harry had accepted that that was a deal, the partnership was bound to last a lifetime. In his mind he divorced Christine, finally. There was nothing to forgive.

At Banbury, Harry had been about to take on a job, temporary, he assured himself, as gaff-lad on a Moon-rocket, when he came upon Sir Henry's advertisement. He was in the Public Library, scanning all the newspaper small-ads, on the lookout, not for a job, but for a Rolls-Royce 'Flying Lady' mascot. His current one had not yet been stolen—it was secured against theft, these days, by a minute Allen screw to which few potential thieves would have a key. But Harry liked the idea of having a spare, even if he had to pay through the nose for it. Dad's three thousand pounds, no longer in the Post Office, with occasional contributions from Harry's own earnings, had quadrupled itself by now. So it was the words 'Rolls-Royce experience an asset' that had leapt out of the page at Harry. And he knew a lying-down gaff when he saw one.

Sir Henry, it turned out, didn't actually own a Rolls-Royce, so it was not this that turned the trick. More probably, thought Harry, that wonderful reference from Brigadier Lord Somebody. However, Sir Henry did have, in the garage, a 1954 Bentley Standard Steel saloon. He seldom used it, preferring to motor to and from London in a comfortable Rover 2000. But Harry's 'Rolls-Royce experience'—a phrase which Sir Henry had seen in other similar advertisements, and which seemed to lend tone to his own—was not wasted. It turned out that the Bentley's engine was almost identical, in principle, to that of Harry's Rolls-Royce. Harry was able, without having to learn his way around a new engine, to tune and restore the Bentley to such good condition that Sir Henry, on his weekends in the country, could confidently and proudly use it to visit those few of his landowning neighbours as had admitted him to their acquaintance. This did Harry no end of good. It was in his chauffeur/handyman period, before Sir Henry had discovered Harry's typewriting skill, his literacy, and a surprising commercial sharpness in such matters as the relative cost

and nutritive value of different types of hen food, and had con-
ceived of his self-enhancing idea, the possession of an 'Estate
Steward'. On his appointment to the important-sounding post
Harry had been told, 'I regard you now, Harry, as a—er,
er,—a junior officer. The other men I regard as—er—as men.'
Harry was, in fact, the greatest find Sir Henry had had in
the creation of his feudal dream. One day someone might
call him 'Squire'. If that ever happened, much of the credit
would be Harry's. His Weekly Reports were solid evidence of
this.

As much of this personal history as Harry deemed understand-
able, and not too discreditable to himself, he related to
Maureen and Albert in the apple-pressing room. This spacious
area of the outbuildings, though not used for cider-making for
forty years, kept about it the rich aroma of fermented fruit.
Harry, Maureen and Albert reclined on the pine floor beside
the press.

'I was never a spieler, you see,' Harry told Albert, as if this
accusation had been the whole occasion of his autobiographical
outpouring, 'though I did do a spell in a tent as back-up to a
Great World Events spieler. He wasn't much good, the spieler,
the flatties saw through him. Could have done it better myself,
but never did.'

'Still,' said Albert with satisfaction, 'I got you bang to rights,
didn't I?'

'You did,' Harry acknowledged.

'Albert always knew,' said Maureen. 'I never believed him,
meself. Begob, I t'ought you was the grand one!'

''Ve ony fing vat puzzles me,' said Albert, laying it on a bit, 'is
your voice. You're no Londoner.'

'No. But my circus had been East End based, originally. So
had Christine's fair. There's a lot of trade between the
showmen and the smoke. I picked it up, I guess.'

'So what's your real voice?' Albert asked. The question

sounded quite urgent. Harry thought hard. He wanted to give a truthful answer, and did.

'Haven't got one,' he said. Maureen made a sound that conveyed sorrow and sympathy. 'What about you?' he asked Albert, obviously not referring to his voice.

'Oh, me,' said Albert, dismissing himself, 'Maureen knows all about me, didn't she say?'

'Not a dicky bird.'

Albert looked at Maureen appreciatively. 'I'm on the run,' he said. 'Armed robbery. Got out of the Isle of Wight years ago.'

'Were you guilty?' asked Harry.

'Not very guilty, no,' said Albert, surprised that he should be asked. 'A bit of robbery, maybe, but no arms. I got done for someone else's.'

'How did you get the job here?'

'Read a book,' said Albert. '*How to Breed Game Birds*. Got it out the library. Not many people know how to breed game. Sir Henry doesn't know nuffing. When I got here he'd got about six old pheasant on the estate. Him and his pals had shot at them so often they couldn't get off the ground, they was so full of lead. Ruined their sex lives, too, they couldn't lay an egg between them. But look around now. When Sir Henry drives off to London in his big black car, and he sees these great healthy-looking brown birds getting up off the verges, he thinks, them birds is *my* birds, I could invite King George the Fifth down out of Heaven, if I wanted, to blast the buggers to smithereens. He likes that. I tell you, I'm safe as houses here. So long you two keep your traps.'

'You're a right pair, you are,' said Maureen happily.

'You're not so bad yourself, Mave,' said Harry, interpreting her comment as favourable.

Albert sucked his teeth sceptically. 'Well, it can't last forever, can it? Stands to reason. But we can 'ave a good rest for a bit, can't we?'

'I'd drink to that,' said Harry, 'if suitable drink were available.'

'Just listen to that,' said Maureen. 'He doesn't half do it a treat.'

Mention of drink reminded Albert that he had a flagon of cider concealed in one of the adjacent outbuildings. He had no intention of turning up at Sir Henry's staff party stone cold sober. He didn't think there was enough cider to spread usefully among three, or even two, so he evidenced an urgent need for a pee and slipped cautiously through the huge double doors of the apple-pressing room.

Maureen's immediate impulse was to move further away from Harry, but she suppressed it, feeling that breathlessness again, and the pleasurable fear. Maureen knew that here, in England, her virginity would be regarded by other girls of her advanced age as unbelievable; or, if believed, possibly as shameful, certainly as funny. She also knew that one day she would have to 'do it', marriage or no marriage, and indeed looked forward with as much dreamy anticipation as awed apprehension to that day. But it would be a day of her choosing, in circumstances of her choosing, with the man of her choice. All three considerations would have to be met. She wasn't going to be rolled by surprise, not even by somebody she thought she quite possibly loved. Not even by Harry. However, she didn't move away from him.

They were sitting with their backs against the solid brick base of the apple press, their legs stretched out in front of them across sweetly smelling pine. Harry had to admit that Maureen's legs were not in absolutely the top class; not as good as Isobel's, though they were better than Lady Luke's, whose handsome knees were let down by too sharp shinbones, ankles too thin and bony. Maureen's were simply a bit muscular for Harry's taste. However, he recognised that to allow these on the whole aesthetic considerations to be a major factor in forming sexual attachments, as in the case of Christine, was absurd. Mave's legs, he decided, were absolutely okay, for a small person; and the rest of her person pleased him enormously. Her merry, enthusiastic, inquisitive blue eyes were particularly attractive. What she was like inside this pleasing exterior he had no idea. He knew very little about her, but felt sure she was a good person. He could hardly enjoy her company so much if she were not. Her sexual nervousness he regarded with sympathetic amusement. She could hardly be expected to put out like Isobel.

'Your turn, Mave,' said Harry.

'Hey! What do you mean?'

'I give you a bit of me, you give me a bit of you, tit for tat, pat. How long you been here?'

'Oh, that!' said Maureen, relieved. *Give me a bit of you* had alarmed her for a moment. 'Well, let's see, two years, just short of. My first post in England, I came straight from Kerry. Her ladypip put an ad in the *Irish Times*. She came all the way out to Kenmare to interview me. On an airyplane. I couldn't believe my luck.'

'What was so lucky?' asked Harry.

'Well, the terms were good, and I was to get my own room with a tee-vee set and all. Nice and near London, that was exciting—not that I've had a chance to go near the flipping place—and best of all, she didn't frighten me, she didn't seem grand at all, just rich. I didn't realise, then, what an eejit she is really, but that's no matter. Still, I nearly left, just before you came. I would have left, I think, if you hadn't.'

'Why?'

'Well, it's so *boring*, Harry! There was no one to speak to, before you came, except Albert, and he doesn't speak much. He's nice, but he's a loner. And down the village it's all deadly dull. I went in the pub once, had me heart in me mouth but I needn't have worried. It was crammed with all these flash London types, drinking vodka tonics and shouting at each other. Young men with no beard to their cheeks and spotted hankies tucked into open-necked shirts and girls in tight pants that showed the line of their knickers across their buttocks and fancy T-shirts that said *I'm Diana—Fly Me* across their dainty little bosies. I couldn't believe it, I thought I was watching some tee-vee send-up of the English middle classes. There was nobody there for me, I never bothered with the place again. I don't think there's anyone real in that village at all.'

'Well, there are some,' said Harry, 'but you wouldn't have met them, 'cos I invented 'em—like Mrs Melford, who solves all the crime in the village, and Dan Lawson, who commits it.' Maureen let this unintelligable remark slide past, making a faint mental note for future enquiry. Harry had opened the gates for her, she wasn't about to be diverted by his fantasies.

'And then it's so spooky here, ye know,' Maureen went on. 'Nothing's for real up here at the Hall either. Lady Luke's just a secretary who married the boss. And Sir Henry isn't gentry, I worked for real gentry in Ireland, I can tell the difference. He may be chairman of United Brick, and a millionaire and a Sir, but when he's not here he's just an ordinary businessman, and when he is here, he's a joke. Real gentry don't have ladies' maids and kitchen staff and market gardens and gamekeepers and estate stewards. They can't afford it, they spend all their money trying to keep the rain out of their family homes. I mean, what's this place *for*, Harry? Sir Henry and her ladypip haven't got a flipping family, except for that prostitute Isobel, and she only comes down here once in a blue moon to keep tabs on the millions. See what I mean, Harry? This place—it's all in Sir Henry's *mind*. I don't like that, being a cardboard cut-out in someone else's fil-um. It's spooky. What do you think?'

Harry thought many things. He was deeply impressed by Maureen's sudden impassioned tirade, and convinced that, with a little literate help (his own? well, why not?) she probably could write a novel, even a novel about sex. She had observation and imagination, which he took to be the major requirements of that art. He thought, too, about his own role in helping to flesh out Sir Henry's imaginary world, and found he could make no ethical judgement about that. He had, he told himself, simply responded sympathetically to a felt need. He wanted to give satisfaction, to hold on for a while to a truly cushy gaff. He felt that Maureen would disapprove, as Isobel had done. This confused his feelings about Maureen.

'I think,' Harry said slowly, 'that in your terms I'm a bit spooky myself, so I'm in no position to criticise spookiness in others.'

This made Maureen laugh. In fact, exaggerating her amusement, she fell about a bit, one of her falls accidentally resulting in her head touching Harry's shoulder. Harry, in order to share her hilarity more closely, swung his arm around and held her head there. Maureen made no effort to change her position, but at once became serious. 'No, Harry,' she said, 'no, you're not spooky. What you are is . . . what you are is . . .'

'What am I, Mave? Come on!'

'What you are, Harry, is, you're a throw-back. A throw-back, that's what you are.'

Harry could only agree, but had to satisfy himself on one point. 'Does that matter,' he asked, 'to you?'

'Oh no,' said Maureen, rubbing the top of her curly head against Harry's chin, 'I love you the way you are.'

A few kisses later, pressed as much by time as by Harry's need to distance himself from Maureen's body, they pushed away from each other and stood up. Harry looked at Maureen happily. 'I don't know about you,' he said, 'but I'll show you how I feel.' He straightened his back, bent his knees, and did a perfect back-flip. Maureen was amazed. 'Here!' she said. 'Can you do that again?' 'No,' said Harry, 'but I can do this.' He raised his arms, leant slowly sideways, and cartwheeled in a circle, with Maureen, turning and applauding, at its centre.

'It's a treat, the way you do that,' she said, as Harry straightened his clothes and ran fingers through his hair. 'Will you do that for me again some day?'

'When I'm in the mood, Mave, when I'm in the mood,' said Harry.

They slipped out together through the double doors, Maureen making for her room to compose herself with lipstick and a stiff hair brush, Harry for the Estate Office. He felt an urgent need to check the content of his recently completed Weekly Report.

Harry glanced at his watch, wondering whether he had time partially to re-type the Weekly Report so as to exclude the only fictitious element it contained. Glancing through it he had confirmed that it was fuller than usual of concrete domestic events. He doubted if Albert's head-count of game available for slaughter at the Boxing Day Shoot were anything but a wild guess, but that was Albert's fiction, not Harry's. The poor egg returns, he hoped he had made clear without being offensive, were a direct result of Sir Henry's refusal to have the underfloor heating of the deep litter house switched on until there was snow on the ground. The big news of the week, satisfyingly redolent of the rustic way of life, was Len's discovery of a badgers' sett in the scrub-covered earthworks that everybody called, without a scrap of evidence, 'the Roman Fort'. This was at the very edge of Sir Henry's small domain, which at this point briefly 'marched with', as Sir Henry liked to put it, the much larger estate of Sir Piers Hamilton. Sir Piers, a baronet with connections among the Irish nobility, lived the life of a recluse in a small Elizabethan mansion several miles beyond the village which he had once owned. Any hopes Sir Henry might have entertained of making friends with his well-connected neighbour had long since withered away, but he enjoyed an occasional reminder of Sir Piers's existence, which Harry from time to time contrived to supply. This week the discovery of the badgers' sett provided him with an excuse for a short anecdote about that ubiquitous village villain 'Dan Lawson', being discovered in one of Sir Piers's copses with a dead partridge stuffed down the top of each wellington boot, a net concealed under his ragged waistcoat . . . It wasn't much of a story, but it combined the elements Sir Henry most relished within a context which was itself verifiable. Harry re-read it now with twinges of doubt, even of guilt, which nothing Isobel said could have provoked. It was, however, too interconnected with the previous story to be excised without much re-typing. Harry decided to leave it. He threw the carbon copy with some irritation on top of the now jumbled pile of papers in his filing basket, looked at his watch again, and decided to go and deliver the top copy to Sir Henry's study. It was twelve fifteen. Only a quarter of an hour to go to the party.

Harry passed through the service door cautiously. Len and Bobby were enthusiastically piling logs on to the fire Len had built inside the vast open fire-place. It was an impressive sight, and although it contributed virtually nothing to heating the hall, at least it looked warm. On the refectory table snowy white table napkins covered the sweet and savoury titbits that Gerda had prepared. Further down the table a neat row of labelled parcels, wrapped in discreetly patterned paper, was lined up with military precision in the exact centre of the long oak board. As Harry passed through the hall towards the study Lady Luke emerged from her drawing-room bearing a vase full of chrysanthemums. She was followed by Maureen, carrying another.

'I'll put mine over here, Maureen,' she said over her shoulder. 'You put yours down the other end.'

'Yes, ma'am,' said Maureen, avoiding Harry's eye. When Lady Luke saw Harry she said, 'Ah, Harry, there you are, I know there was something I wanted to ask you . . .' she put down the vase and fished a list from the waistband of her skirt.

'I must just go and put the Weekly Report on Sir Henry's desk, Lady Luke,' said Harry, not pausing in his passage down the hall.

'No, wait a minute, let me see . . .' Lady Luke scanned her list anxiously, chewing the side of her lower lip. By the time she said 'Ah yes!' and looked up, Harry had gone.

In Sir Henry's study, the door of which was opposite that of Lady Luke's drawing-room, Harry found Isobel. It was pleasantly warm in here, the central heating set a notch higher than elsewhere. Isobel was reclining in a deep leather-upholstered armchair and leafing through a copy of *Shooting Times and Country Magazine* without deep interest. She was wearing tights now, against the biting cold in the unheatable hall. Harry acknowledged that they enhanced the fine lines of her legs, while regretting the disappearance of that little fuzz of down on either side of her knee-caps. Then, remembering his new resolution, and his growing attachment to Maureen, set such thoughts aside.

'You'll catch it if Sir Henry knows you've been in here,' said Harry.

'He won't,' said Isobel, 'unless you tell him. You could always put it in next week's report I suppose.'

Harry ignored that, crossing to the desk and arranging his pages of typescript in one corner of Sir Henry's blotter, aligning their edges immaculately with the edges of the pad.

'Delivering the weekly short story?'

'Entirely factual this week,' Harry assured her.

'Like hell it is. Say that again.'

'What? Why?'

'What you just said. I want to hear it.'

'Look, Isobel, why don't you . . . Oh hell, why not? Entirely factual this . . .'

'Yes, I thought so,' said Isobel, interrupting. 'You know, there's a definite note of cockney in your voice sometimes. You said "fac'ule". A Welshman would have said "fac-tu-al".'

'Balls,' said Harry. 'I've never been further into London than Hampstead Heath F . . . for a quick visit.'

Isobel made a grimace which Harry couldn't interpret. In Isobel's social circle it was known as making-a-that-sucks-mouth.

'Have you read Uncle Henry's blotter?' she said.

'Read his blotter?'

'You know—holding it up to the mirror so you can see what he's been scribbling.'

Harry looked at the blotter. Sir Henry used an old-fashioned fountain pen, not a biro, and the blotter was covered with spidery hieroglyphs.

'Of course not!' said Harry, in a shocked voice. 'That would be a rotten thing to do.'

'Oh, don't be so weird. You poke about among his pornography.'

'That's different.'

'I can't see why.'

Harry couldn't explain why, but felt convinced that it was so. Isobel didn't consider the issue worth her attention. 'He's got a girl in Islington,' she said, snuffling with suppressed laughter, 'who dresses up for him in kinky gear. He describes some new stuff he's having sent to her from a mail-order house as if she's going to be thrilled. I bet she'd rather have the cash.'

'What sort of stuff?' Harry couldn't help asking.

'Oh, you know, open-crotch panties, bras with holes for the nipples to come through, you know the kind of thing.'

Harry didn't. He knew what strippers were prepared to go down to in the Fairs, but he hadn't encountered these inventions and couldn't see the point of them. He felt vaguely dirty for having allowed himself to be sucked into this conversation.

'I wonder what they actually *do*?' Isobel mused. Then she thought of something else and laughed again. 'Oh yes,' she said, 'and he's hooked on speed. I wouldn't have guessed that, would you?'

'Don't you ever feel disloyal, Isobel?' Harry asked, wondering what 'speed' was.

'Don't you ever feel like a pompous prick, Harry?' said Isobel lightly. She got out of the deep armchair, her skirt riding high up her thighs. 'Better go,' she said. 'Time for joy and the true spirit of Christmas. Take a peek outside, Harry.'

Harry opened the door a crack and peered out. Lady Luke wasn't in sight. They went out into the dark anteroom that led to the hall. From here they could see Lady Luke at the mullioned window beside the porch door, peering up the drive for a sight of her husband's car. 'See you later,' said Isobel in a low voice, and slipped into the drawing-room opposite. Harry emerged into the hall and coughed. Lady Luke turned from the window.

'Oh, Harry, good!' she said, as if congratulating him on being there at just the right moment. 'Will you check that they're all ready back there? Sir Henry won't want to be kept waiting once he arrives.'

'Of course, Lady Luke,' said Harry, relieved that lists, and his failure to assist with their completion, now seemed to be forgotten.

In the kitchen Gerda and Hans were locked in animated, loving conversation, in German. Mrs Pantry presided aloofly, somehow making it clear to everybody that this was her kitchen and they had better be on their best behaviour. Maureen and Albert were muttering together in a corner, with Bobby hovering nearby in the hope of getting close to Maureen. A pimply youth called Alex, from the office of the estate agents in Great Dunmow who paid all their wages and stamped their National Insurance cards, was standing around looking awkward, with good reason. Nobody knew how he had first managed to promote himself as one having a right to attend these occasions, but after three or four years of doing so he seemed to have established it as a custom. Len and Pantry were absent.

'Where's Len?' Harry asked at large, having counted heads.

'Gone out to look at his cabbage patch,' said Albert.

'Mr Pantry,' said Mrs Pantry, full of dignity, 'said not to expect him until the last moment.'

Rotten little creep, thought Harry. He went off to look for Len, who turned out to be having a leisurely piss on some turnips of his own growing. In the cold winter air the steam of Len's urine reached Harry's nostrils as the smell of burnt iron filings, somehow rather invigorating.

'Don't forget,' said Harry to Len, 'to tell them about Spot's fight with the rat.'

'Ah, no, Mister Harry,' said Len, 'not iffen you make 'at easy for me.'

''At's a good story, Len, the way you told 'at to me,' said Harry, slipping easily into Len's voice, which Len only subliminally noticed. He could 'get on with' Harry, but couldn't quite say why, the young man being such a come-far foreigner.

'We's better go in,' said Harry, but Len wouldn't be hurried, buttoning the many fly-buttons of his best doe-skin trousers with infuriating slowness. Back in the kitchen Harry found Gerda, Maureen and Alex all absent. Nervousness had sent them all to the lavatories. 'You'd better make sure you're all present and correct when I come for you,' said Harry with a tone of authority that made Mrs Pantry sniff. He went back down the service corridor with unsettled emotions. This was his first Christmas here. He was unsure of the drill.

In the great hall Harry found Lady Luke, a lonely figure, still at her vigil before the mullioned window. No sign of Isobel, no doubt deeply immersed in back copies of *Vogue*. Harry went to stand beside his employer's nervous wife.

'It's all alright, Lady Luke,' he said gently. 'Everything's been done that needs doing, the staff are all assembled in the kitchen, and it's still only twenty-eight minutes past twelve.'

Lady Luke gripped his elbow with desperate fingers. 'Oh, Harry,' she cried, 'you *are* such a help!' No trace of the 'well-fuck-you' attitude of earlier in the morning. Harry's heart melted a little further. 'Look, Celia,' he said, 'don't *worry* so much. Nobody's going to blame you if the timing goes haywire, we can all see the problem, there's nothing you can do about it.'

She squeezed his elbow so tightly it was painful.

'Bless you, Harry,' she said, 'bless you!'

They stared out of the green-tinted glass together at the bleak winter world. Harry would have liked to have found further consoling words for Lady Luke, to whom he at the moment felt he was often unjustifiably beastly. He was in a Pierrot mood, he recognised that. But further consolation suddenly became unnecessary. 'Oh, look, Harry, look!' The glossy black car swung importantly around the circular flower bed in front of the Hall and scrunched to a halt in a spurt of gravel. Lady Luke took her hand away from Harry's elbow. There was a long pause. The shadowy figure in the car seemed to Harry to be eating something from the palm of his cupped hand. Then the driver's door opened and Sir Henry appeared, a small plump person in a dark-blue chalk-striped suit, clutching a briefcase, umbrella and bowler hat. The latter he at once used to cover his thin silver hair. He reached back inside the car and dragged out a heavy dark grey top-coat, then slammed the Rover's door. As if by magic the loosely suited figure of Pantry appeared beside him. They conferred, Sir Henry moving his feet restlessly.

'Oh my God,' said Lady Luke. 'Fucking Pantry!'

'Nothing I could have done, Celia,' said Harry. 'The stinking little sod's got a bee in his bonnet.'

'Yes, and you know who'll suffer?' said Lady Luke with bitter conviction. '*Me*, that's who!'

Harry said nothing, sensing the truth of this. Lady Luke took hold of his elbow again and shook it. 'It's not your fault, darling, it's not your fault.'

Shaken by that 'darling'—was she consolidating her gains while the moment lasted, or was it a habit from her past?— Harry could do no more than mutter 'Stinking little sod!' again. It seemed to be enough. It even made her briefly smile.

Sir Henry shook himself free of Pantry irritably and advanced on the great iron-studded door of his castle. Lady Luke darted quickly towards the porch door. She caught him there, between one oak and the other, and her thin cry drifted back to Harry on the bitter breeze that swept through the hall: 'Who's a good, good, *good* boy!' Embarrassed, he retreated down the hall and took up a position, hands behind back, to one side of the roaring fire. His eyes met those of some unknown person's ancestor. Harry winked at him.

'Give me five minutes, Harry,' said Sir Henry, bustling past. 'Five minutes. Then bring them all in.'

'Very good, Sir Henry.' Harry watched his employer leaping speedily up the main staircase, wondering where he got his energy from, and then himself disappeared through the service door, heading for the kitchen. Here all was in order although boredom had set in, occasioning silly jokes. 'What they having for Christmas dinner, Mrs Pantry?' asked Albert, now slightly drunk. 'Roast brick?' Everyone thought this very funny except Mrs Pantry and Gerda, who had to have it explained to her. 'Chairman of the United Brick Company, see? Roast brick!' Under pressure from this typically British humour Gerda went into hysterics, to the evident fury of Hans, who shouted commands at her in German. Pantry came into the kitchen furtively, avoiding Harry's eye. Harry, feeling that this was no moment for putting questions of precedence to the test, said in a loud voice, 'Mr Pantry, why don't you and Mrs Pantry lead us in? I'll bring up the rear.' To Albert he said, sideways, 'Stay close, Albert.'

'Wiv you, cock,' said Albert.

'Over to you, then, Mr Pantry,' said Harry, glancing at his watch. 'It's time.' Pantry, undone by Harry's deft footwork, could find nothing to complain about. He marginally changed the order behind him, preferring Alex, the estate agents's lad, to follow Mrs Pantry rather than the much more senior Len. Then they moved in self-conscious procession down the service corridor to the great hall.

Sir Henry was already in possession. He had exchanged his suit jacket for a soft black velvet smoking jacket, his severe club tie for a flamboyant polka-dotted bow. He usually dressed in tweeds on his country weekends, but clearly on this occasion there had been no time for a complete change. The effect of the combination of bow tie, velvet jacket and chalk-stripe trousers was bizarre; even, Harry found, poignant. Sir Henry. had provided himself with a large cigar and a huge glass of amber fluid, both of which he held, at the moment, in the same hand.

He stood straddled before the blazing log fire, stroking his bottom to rub the heat in.

Pantry knew what to do. He led his little procession in such a way that, when he halted it, they formed a shallow ellipse of which the two stone columns on either side of the fire-place were the dual foci. Once this was established Pantry, and then by example Harry, shuffled forward a little, drawing their respective wings of the ellipse nearer to the fire, and to their employer. Behind them, at the refectory table, Isobel was pouring sherry. Gerda made a move towards the table as if to whip away the protective napkins from the food she had prepared, but was shooed back into line by Lady Luke. 'No, no, Gerda, today I am *your* servant!' she cried. Harry indicated that he could help Isobel hand round the sherry glasses. Handing him a glass, Isobel whispered, 'No, no, Harry, today I am *your* . . .'

'Oh, yeah?' whispered Albert, rather loudly, at Harry's elbow. 'Goings on?'

When they were all served with sherry Sir Henry held his own different drink aloft. Muttering among the staff dwindled to silence.

'Well, my old friends and colleagues,' said Sir Henry, 'here I am again amongst you at yet another Christmas gathering, to wish you all on behalf of myself and Lady Luke all the best sentiments of the Christmas season, and may we all look forward to another happy and productive year's work together!'

'I'll drink to that,' said Pantry emphatically. He sipped his sherry, held it up to the light to admire its colour and clarity, then closed his eyes with an air of sumptuous well-being. They all drank. Sir Henry clearly thought it was now time for general conversation. 'Well Albert,' he said jovially, 'what sort of a week did you have, eh? Busy?'

'Not so bad, sir,' said Albert evasively.

'Pullets laying well?'

'Fair to middling, sir.'

'You'll have been doing a head-count on the game birds for Boxing Day I imagine?'

'That's about it, sir.'

'Cold work, eh?'

'Oh, I dunno, sir. Work's much of a muchness. All bad.'

The assembled company roared appreciatively at this sally of Albert's, which he would not have made if he'd been entirely sober. But Sir Henry didn't laugh, and Harry thought this the right moment for a diversion. He leant forward so as to address Len at the other end of the ellipse. 'I say, Len,' he called across the empty space, 'have you told Sir Henry and Lady Luke about Spot's fight with the rat?'

'What!' cried Sir Henry. 'Not *Spot*!'

'Not fighting with a rat!' cried Lady Luke.

'Ah,' said Len reminiscently, ' 'at were a real funny fight, 'at were.' He told the story very slowly, with a wealth of circumstantial detail and a vivid account of Spot's physical gyrations, but omitted to mention the humorous point of the story, which was that the rat had been dead for some time before Spot found it and began to fight with it. Harry had told the story, succinctly and with a decent sense of dramatic timing, to Lady Luke only a few days previously, and had nothing but admiration for her cries of wonder as the long, dull chronicle unfolded. 'Well,' she breathed, 'I just wouldn't have thought old Spot had it in him!'

There now arose a dispute, eagerly fanned from all sides, as to whether Spot was or was not a better gun-dog than Sally, recently deceased. Pantry, who had never in his life attended a shoot, dominated the argument. Isobel, pausing in front of Harry with a platter of prunes wrapped in fried bacon, remarked, 'Feeling particularly doggy today then, are we?'

'Thank you, Miss Isobel,' said Harry, taking a prune.

Lady Luke now began distributing presents, a late chorus of oohs and aahs echoing along the line as wrapping paper was stripped away to reveal the gifts. Sir Henry followed her, shaking hands. Harry, a non-smoker, received his own box of

Benson and Hedges with a little bow. Then Sir Henry was upon him. 'Ah, Harry,' he said as he shook hands. 'Your first Christmas among us, eh? Let's hope it'll be the first of many!' Dropping his voice, Sir Henry added, 'Can you spare a few minutes in the study when this is over?'

'Of course, Sir Henry,' said Harry, thinking, a few hours if you like, old cock. Christmas Eve meant nothing to Harry. His dinner next day would be a fillet steak from the freezer compartment of his calor-gas refrigerator in the caravan. He had no social plans for today.

Sir Henry returned to his pivotal position before the fire. Isobel came to stand beside Harry.

'Slip me those fags, will you?' she asked, whispering.

'How much?'

'What do you want?' Not 'how much', but 'what'. Well, he'd said he liked his wenches brazen. 'You can have them,' said Harry, 'and I'll . . .'

'Yes?'

At this moment Pantry commenced heavily upon the loyal toast. 'I just want to say,' he said, as if at the end of a long session of bargaining, 'that me and Mrs Pantry, and all the staff here I think I can safely say, greatly appreciate your hospitality, Sir Henry, Lady—er—Luke, and the fine conditions under which we—er—work for you, and we all, all of us here, wish you all the very best of, er, luck, and, er, prosperity, in the coming year, and may next Christmas be, be, as happy as this Christmas.'

Pantry raised his nearly empty glass. 'To Sir Henry and Lady-er-Luke!' he cried. 'Long may they—er—live!'

The staff sipped at the dregs of their glasses. Albert nudged Harry. 'Freeza,' he said. Harry took a step forward and turned to face the expectant faces of the staff. He had an excellent tenor voice, and could hit a note first time off. 'Fo-o-o-o-r,' he sang, one arm rising above his head. They didn't let him down.

'For he's a jolly good fellow!' they all sang. Sir Henry basked in the collective love of his estate's staff. 'Unbelievable!'

muttered Isobel beside Harry. He ignored her and sang on. The whole thing, he found was peculiarly stimulating. 'You buy this?' asked Isobel, below the singing. 'Absolutely,' said Harry, taking breath.

'You are so *weird!*' said Isobel.

Sir Henry, with a fresh glass of whisky on the desk before him and the still viable remains of his cigar smouldering between plump, hairy knuckles, was reading the last page of the Weekly Report when Harry, after knocking, entered the study. Sir Henry waved him to the leather armchair. He seemed to Harry to spend an unnaturally long time reading the three-quarters of a page of typescript. Harry began to feel an unfocused anxiety. Finally Sir Henry laid the page down on top of the others, shuffled the edges neatly together, and turned them over. He took off his glasses, knuckled each eye in turn, and sighed.

'Harry,' he said heavily, 'you have made the most *appalling* blunder.'

'Eh?' said Harry. 'I've done what?' For a moment he entertained a wild suspicion: somehow, somewhere, Sir Henry had at last made the acquaintance of his neighbour Sir Piers Hamilton; quite naturally they had at once fallen to exchanging anecdotes about 'Dan Lawson' and 'Mrs Melford' . . . No. Harry shook his head to rid it of such nonsense.

'Whatever possessed you,' said Sir Henry slowly, '*to tell Pantry what the timber merchant said?* You must have been out of your mind!'

Harry felt a wave of relief. It was simple enough after all. He said carefully, 'I'm afraid I don't quite understand you, Sir Henry. Pantry saw Mr Hobhouse inspecting the elm. Naturally, when he asked me what the verdict was, I told him.'

'Do you realise,' said Sir Henry patiently, as if explaining to a child that a burning coal tends to be hot, 'that Pantry won't give me a moment's peace, now, until that elm has been removed?'

'Well, sir, it will have to *be* removed, won't it? I mean, I wouldn't have asked for an expert opinion if it hadn't already shown signs of being in a dangerous condition. Hobhouse simply confirmed what we already suspected.'

'What *you* suspected, Harry,' corrected Sir Henry quietly, 'you and that hysterical old woman Pantry. How many other *expert* opinions have you had?'

'There hasn't been time to get more than one. I've treated it as a matter of urgency, and I should have thought . . .'

'I don't belive you've done any thinking on the subject at all, Harry,' snapped Sir Henry. 'How many times have I told you that nothing on this estate—absolutely *nothing*—is to be sold without first getting two or more offers for it?'

Sir Henry had never spoken to Harry in tones like this before. He was quite formidable, yet Harry was not intimidated, sustained as he was by the first stirrings of a virtuous anger.

'I think I explained in my report, sir,' he said evenly, 'that Hobhouse is not interested in the elm unless he can have it next week. He is the only timber merchant in the district, it might be months before I could persuade another one to come here from even further away. By that time the sap will have started rising and they won't want to touch the tree until October at the earliest. And you must know, Sir Henry, that dying elms are two a penny round here these days. You told me yourself—and everyone confirms it—that we can expect the worst gales in January and February. I should have thought it was self-evident that the tree should be removed while we have the chance.'

Sir Henry listened to all this attentively, sucking one ear-hook of his spectacles and gazing at the intricately carved oak panelling behind Harry's head. 'You would have thought it self-evident would you, Harry?' he murmured thoughtfully. 'It's a pity that it was not self-evident to you that this Hobhouse thought—quite correctly—that he was on to a soft touch.'

'How do you mean, sir?'

'Unlike you, Harry, this man is a businessman. His job is to make money, not to give free advice to ignorant amateurs. Put yourself in his position. It must have been as clear to him as it is to me that you know next to nothing about forestry. I've no doubt he spun you a long tale about the various tests he could make to see how much of the tree was still alive and in sound condition. Am I right?'

'Quite right, sir,' said Harry uneasily.

'Right. So he then proceeded to apply these tests. Not unnaturally—if you remember his main object in life—the so-called tests showed that the tree was rotten right through, precariously held from falling across Pantry's cottage by a single root which might at any moment prove to be over-burdened. Right?'

'Right.'

'Our friend then makes a great show of being reluctant to have anything to do with the tree. He points out how difficult it is going to be to get the tree down without damaging the surrounding buildings. He demonstrates that it will take two tractors and at least six men, and he gives a terrifying estimate of the cost of such an operation. When you say that the tree must be worth a good deal as timber, he reminds you that it is rotten right through and he might well find himself landed, after all that trouble and expense, with nothing but a worthless, hollow shell.'

Harry was appalled. Sir Henry had traced, with almost supernatural accuracy, the exact course of the transaction between himself and Mr Hobhouse. He sat motionless in his chair, quivering slightly, like a rabbit in mid-field mysteriously transfixed by myxomatosis.

'But then,' Sir Henry continued quietly, examining his spotless fingernails for possible blemishes, 'having reduced you to a state in which you would agree to practically anything in order to be rid of that terrible tree, out of the kindness of his heart and because he doesn't like to see a decent bloke in a difficult position, he agrees to take a chance on it. He offers you a token payment of twenty pounds for the timber, although he expects, when he gets the tree down, that he'll find he's making a loss on the deal. You are lucky, he says, that he has in fact got a market for a small quantity of unseasoned elm next week, and he can probably salvage enough from this rotten old tree to meet his client's requirements. But if he can't have it next week, he doesn't want it at all. And he warns you that if you don't sell it pretty quickly, you won't be able to sell it until October—a fact, Harry, which is very likely untrue. The truth is,' said Sir Henry, leaning forward and tapping Harry's Weekly Report to demonstrate where the truth wasn't, 'the *truth* is, Hobhouse's tests have shown him, if anything, what he can see perfectly well with his naked eye, that the disease has so far only attacked a few branches on one side of the tree and that the rest of it is perfectly sound and probably worth, as timber, something like three hundred pounds. Has he rung you up yet to ask for my go-ahead?'

'Yes,' said Harry.

'Shows he's keen,' said Sir Henry. He shifted his bottom in his chair; selected, pierced and lit a new cigar; then sat back, tasting the smoke critically, to wait for whatever Harry might find to say.

It took a little while, as Harry floundered among weak alternatives, for him to find a line he thought he could sustain. At length he said slowly, 'That's all very well, Sir Henry. It may well be that Mr Hobhouse is, as you suggest, dishonest and a blatant liar—though you have no real grounds for the supposition . . .'

'One moment!' cried Sir Henry, holding up one plump hand, palm outwards, like a policeman on point duty. 'I did not suggest that he was dishonest and a blatant liar, Harry. I simply pointed out that he was a businessman and could be expected to behave like one.'

'If that's what businessmen . . .' Harry began to cry hotly, but, realising that this was likely to be an unproductive point to make, swallowed the rest of his sentiment. Sir Henry allowed

himself a bleak little smile. Harry tried again. 'I still say that
you may be slandering Hobhouse, sir, he struck me as a very
decent type of man, but *even if you aren't*, even if he is as deceitful
as you think, I still say that he should be given the go-ahead to
take the tree out next week.'

'Oh? And how do you reach that interesting conclusion,
young man?'

'Because there's an element of doubt involved,' Harry said
firmly, feeling that he had at last laid hands on a principle
which would not crumble beneath him. 'We haven't time,
before the bad weather starts, to find out the real facts. The tree
may be unsound, or it may not be. If it stood anywhere else it
wouldn't matter, but where it is, leaning the way it does, even
the slightest suspicion ought to be enough to condemn it
without another thought.'

Sir Henry was genuinely puzzled. 'And throw away, possibly,
two or three hundred pounds?' he asked.

'Certainly,' said Harry with new-found conviction. 'If it did
fall, it would carry away part of the garden wall, both the
workshops and . . .'

Sir Henry leaned forward, his hand raised again. 'Surely,
Harry,' he said gently, 'I don't have to remind you that
everything on this estate is insured? *Everything!*'

'If you had let me finish I was going to say, and end up
crushing the kitchen of Pantry's cottage. A man, a woman, and
three children live in that cottage, Sir Henry.'

Harry felt better now. He had lost his grip for a moment back
there under pressure from Sir Henry's uncanny reconstruction
of events, but nothing Sir Henry could say now, he was
convinced, could shake him from his hold on so obvious a
principle. But what Sir Henry did say shook Harry in a quite
different way.

'Harry,' he said, as if unable to understand Harry's problem,
'Harry, I am insured for damage to persons as well as to
property.'

Harry gaped. 'What—what did you say, sir?'

'I said,' said Sir Henry patiently, 'I am insured for damage to persons as well as to property.'

There was a long silence, during which Harry examined Sir Henry's face carefully, like a lepidopterist puzzling over an unknown species of moth. Then he prized himself out of his chair, feeling suddenly tired.

'I'd better go,' he said.

'That's right, you run along now,' said Sir Henry in sympathetic tones. 'And Harry—don't let it upset you too much. You're not stupid, you'll learn. We've all made mistakes—that's how we learn, by making mistakes. You've done very well, until now, for someone with no training in estate management . . .'

It was Harry's turn to use the raised hand. 'No, Sir Henry,' he said, 'no, you haven't understood. I meant, go from here. Leave. Give in my notice.'

'Oh, don't be so silly, boy, don't be so silly!' said Sir Henry impatiently. 'You want to chuck up a peach of a job like this just because your pride's been damaged a bit? You're making a mountain out of a molehill.'

'No, Sir Henry, it isn't that. It's what you said, about being insured . . . I can't live with that.'

'Oh, nonsense, boy, rubbish, you can't go hiding behind something I said. I quite understand what you're feeling—you're feeling humiliated, that's what it is, but you don't need to, I had no intention of humiliating you, only of teaching you a valuable lesson. I know that when you've had a chance to think about it calmly you'll see I was right to pull you to pieces over a botched job like that. After all,' said Sir Henry, twinkling with amusement, 'it's all blazingly obvious! But we like you, Harry, both of us do. You could settle down to doing a really good job here. And—don't forget this—there *is* room for promotion! Once I'd got to know you a bit better, Harry, over a period, there'd be a strong economic case for taking the wages and National Insurance accounts away from the estate agents and letting you handle them—at, of course, a much enhanced salary! In fact it's the next sensible and obvious move.'

Harry could see that this was indeed so. He could guess the kind of saving that would be made, and, quartering it, the kind of increase in wages he might be offered. He knew that, in a society in which employment of any kind is difficult to find and precarious when found, such a prospect was not to be easily dismissed. He easily dismissed it.

'I'm sorry, Sir Henry, but you said . . .'

'All right, what did I say, what did I say?'

'That you were insured for damage to persons as well as to property.'

'I did. And so I am. Good God, boy, don't you believe me?'

'It isn't that, Sir Henry. You see . . .' But Harry could find no form of words to describe what he himself so clearly saw. Sir Henry got to his feet impatiently, dismissively. 'Do you want me to show you my insurance policies, is that it? Well, I'm sorry, Harry, but if you can't take my word for a thing like that . . .'

'Oh, I do, Sir Henry, I do.'

'Well?'

Harry wished Harlequin would come back, this was so tiring. Sir Henry was staring at him now with irritated, enquiring eyes. His cheeks, Harry noticed, had an unhealthy, purplish flush, his temples were beaded with sweat. Good God, he thought, this one's not long for the world. He hung his head. 'I'm sorry, sir,' he muttered, feeling truly ashamed, resigned to punishment. 'I'd better go.'

'Yes. You're not making a lot of sense, are you? Well, just you think about it, learn your lesson, then put it behind you. We'll start all over on Boxing Day, and see what you can make of things. You'll be at the shoot, won't you? Well, of course you will, we shall need you.'

Harry didn't trust himself to say anything more. He shook his head numbly, dumbly, and left. All he could hear in his head was, No . . . no . . . no . . . no . . . no . . .

'I don't believe it,' said Maureen, beating his chest with her little fists. 'I don't believe it. You *can't* leave! Not after . . .'

After what? A few kisses, a few confidences? 'Mave,' said Harry quietly, 'I *have* to. It wouldn't be decent.'

Maureen clung to him. She didn't want to weep, had kept tears at bay as long as she could. She understood what he had told her, understood that he couldn't stay, and why. She just couldn't accept it. 'And what's to become of me?' she cried; aware that she wasn't, in all fairness, Harry's problem, she added, 'I mean, knowing what I know about the old sod now?'

Harry surprised her by saying soberly, 'Well, Mave, you could come along with me, if you fancied it.'

Maureen checked her emotions and looked at him closely. 'Where to?'

'I don't know. Anywhere.'

'You mean—in the caravan?'

'In the back of the Rolls, if that's what you want. I slept in there until I was fifteen, and grew out of it. It's very comfortable. Just your size.'

'It'd be cold.'

'You'd have to wrap up well. Otherwise—it's the caravan. That's not cold.'

Maureen looked at him challengingly. 'You wouldn't leap on me?' she said fiercely.

'Ah, now,' said Harry, pulling her towards him, 'how can I say that, Mave? I could *try*, I suppose . . . for a while.' Maureen clung to him. He was honest and decent, she said to herself, trembling with fear, honest and decent.

The door of the Estate Office opened and Isobel came in. 'I do beg your pardon,' she said coolly. 'You seem to be rather in demand at the moment, Harry. Celia sent me. She wants you to go and see her in her drawing-room.'

'I was just going,' said Maureen.

Harry said, full of confidence, 'Mave, darling, you needn't. It's all over here. All over. You don't have to do anything you don't want to.'

'I want to wash me face,' said Maureen tightly. 'I'll be back, be sure of it.' She went. Isobel closed the door behind her. She went round behind the desk and played a few notes on the typewriter. 'Don't do that,' said Harry, 'you'll ruin the platen.'

'You are the most god-awful fool,' Isobel said.

'I know that,' said Harry. He didn't want this scene. He was so tired, so tired.

'Look, Harry, it's crazy,' said Isobel without a trace of rancour. 'You've got it made here. Celia's dotty about you. Uncle Henry thinks you just put up an almighty black and so you're suffering from wounded pride and you'll need a day or two to get over it. You do know that, don't you?' she insisted. 'You haven't burned any bridges as far as he's concerned. You'll have come round by Boxing Day and be able to live with your shame.'

'I gathered that was his view,' said Harry. 'It's a mistaken one.'

'Oh don't be so fucking pompous! Why be like that? If Uncle Henry can forgive you for making a fool of yourself, why can't you? Listen, Harry, it isn't just him and you, you know. There's me and you, too. I refuse to take your little thing with that Irish filly seriously. She's not in your class.'

'What class would that be?' asked Harry.

'Not social class, you fool. Oh God.' Isobel sighed. 'Look, Harry, I like you, you know that. All right, I fancy you. You know that too. And you've made it clear enough you fancy me. If you could just get hold of yourself, and drag yourself forward into the last quarter of the twentieth century, you'd be—well, you and I could—Shit! Can't you say something?'

Harry was indeed finding it very difficult to say anything, so he spoke of what he was carefully keeping in the forefront of his mind. 'Do you know what your uncle said to me?'

'No.'

'He said, apropos the danger of the Pantry family being crushed to death by a falling elm tree, that he was insured for damage to persons as well as to property.'

'I see. Well, he would, wouldn't he? You found that unacceptable?'

'Don't you?'

'Harry, it's a question of what people are. Can't you see that? Of course that's what Uncle Henry would say, that's why he's a millionaire. I wouldn't, you wouldn't, poor dear Celia wouldn't, but Uncle Henry would, and did. And you're surprised! Christ, you fucking romantics! Here you are, supporting the poor little money-bag in his country-gentry fantasies, and you don't realise you're supporting him in the other thing too! But you are, you are! And you think you have a right to judge him! You think *you* know the difference between right and wrong, but you don't, Harry. *Nobody does.* What's right for one would be wrong for another. You don't seem to know that. Honestly, Harry, I pity you.'

Harry felt a fog descending over what little he knew of his whispy moral code. He felt undermined, without understanding how a sap had been driven beneath him, what it consisted of. He hadn't set out, he assured himself, no he hadn't, to be a moral arbiter of anything. He could live with some things, not with others. With robbery, but not with armed robbery. With tapping, but not with enforced tapping. Such limits needed no justification, they were felt, not thought. Isobel's clever niceties went by him without touching, yet he still felt undermined.

'You said Celia wanted to see me?'

Isobel looked at him. 'You're not really interested in me, are you? You think I'm shit.'

'I think you have very nice legs,' said Harry, 'and a nifty mind that leaves me trailing. I could never do more than trail, with you. It's not much of a prospect.'

'You're a right eejit,' said Isobel, imitating Maureen. 'I'll be worth millions when the old boy pops off. Not worth trailing along with?'

'That's disgusting,' said Harry, 'the way you say that.'

'That's fucking stupid,' said Isobel, 'the way you say that.'

'I'd better go.'

'Go, little man, go.'

Harry didn't really want to go and see Lady Luke, suspecting that he would be subjected to a lower key version of the enervating scene he had just endured with Isobel. But it was obviously something he could not avoid without seeming, to himself, cowardly, to her, blatantly rude. In the event she surprised him. She was pacing about when he knocked on and opened the door of her drawing-room, and she closed the door quickly when he came in. She knew he was leaving, despite Sir Henry's confidence that he was not, and didn't ask for reasons.

'I never thought you'd last,' she said. 'I hoped you would, oh I did hope you would, because you're the nearest thing to a human being I've met since I came to this bloody place, but I didn't see how you could, knowing the way Henry was about—about things. You weren't very nice to me, but I could see you had to protect your back, and anyway sometimes you were. You really do have to go, do you?'

'I'm afraid so, Celia,' said Harry. 'I didn't really want to, it's been comfortable here, but—well, I just couldn't live with something he said.'

'Don't tell me! Don't tell me!' Lady Luke put her hands over her ears as if protecting herself from words that might destroy her. 'I know. It happens to me all the time. I wish the silly old sod would drop dead.'

Harry gazed at her, wide-eyed. 'Do you really wish that?' he asked.

'Well, not without he changes his will first,' she said savagely, her syntax reverting to that of her native Clapham. 'That bitch Isobel's in for most of it as things stand. God how I hate her!'

'She's not all bad,' said Harry.

'Oh, I know, I know,' said Lady Luke resignedly, 'it's me, I'm a rotten grasping cow myself. At least I didn't have designs on you, the way she did. Not that I couldn't have had, except I can't handle complications. Well, all right, then. Sorry if I ever gave offence, coming the lady.'

'Sorry if I ever gave offence,' said Harry, 'coming the faceless servant.'

Two of a kind, they looked at each other with some hilarity. With enormous relief, Harry could feel Harlequin returning. 'Give us a kiss, then,' she said. Harry gave her a kiss, whole-heartedly. She pushed him away. 'Thanks,' she said. 'Now piss off, I can't afford to have Henry catch you in here. But thanks for coming in to see me. That was brave and—and—well, there you are, you see—human.'

'Hold the door open for me, will you?' asked Harry. She looked puzzled but did as he asked, supposing it some sort of pay-off for his own frequent deferential door-holdings. But it wasn't quite that. To her utter astonishment Lady Luke saw Harry put his hands on the floor in front of him and then raise his legs, with complete and seemingly effortless control, into the air. He walked out of the door into the dark anteroom, and from there into the great hall, now stripped of all traces of Sir Henry's staff party save the smouldering remains of Len's huge fire. Lady Luke followed him out as far as the anteroom's archway and watched as he walked on his hands the entire length of the hall. She began to laugh. When Harry reached the service door he stopped and turned. His head held up, he could see Lady Luke, a tiny figure under the lofty stone arch at the other end of the hall. He could also see, as she could not, that Sir Henry, drawn out of his study by the surprising sound of her laughter, was now standing at her shoulder. Harry waved a leg. Lady Luke waved an arm. 'Bye-bye!' he called, his voice echoing weirdly round the empty spaces of the great hall and the grand staircase. He kicked back at the service door and, when it had swung open, made his upside-down exit, backwards.

'What the devil's going on?' asked Sir Henry. Lady Luke experienced an inexplicable surge of happiness. 'Nothing really, darling,' she said. 'I think Harry's just trying to make a point.'

Harry was frying eggs for himself and Maureen on the small calor-gas stove in the caravan. Maureen was surprised at how spacious the caravan was. The bed, though a double one, didn't dominate it at all—indeed it could be hidden by a curtain. She was sitting comfortably on the banquette beside the table, her elbows on the formica top, fists pushed into flushed cheeks, her mind made up.

'When shall we go?' she asked.

'What's wrong with today?' Harry spooned some hot fat over the egg yolks, to seal them.

'I haven't had me pay.'

'Nor have I. But we're paid a week in advance, remember? If we leave now, we won't be stealing a week's pay.'

'All right,' said Maureen, a bit disappointed. She had rather liked the idea of stealing a week's pay. 'But Harry—what are we going to live on?'

'I've got some money.'

'How much?'

Harry told her. Her eyes widened. 'Hey, Harry, you didn't use that—you could have used that to *entice* me!'

'You didn't need enticing, Mave.'

'No, I didn't, did I?'

Harry looked at her with pleasure and only just saved the toast from burning. He served her with fried eggs, buttered toast, and a fresh tomato stolen from Pantry's greenhouse.

'You won't always have to cook,' said Maureen. 'I can do some things.'

'I should flipping hope so,' said Harry. He enjoyed using Maureen's euphemistic swearwords.

'Are you going to help me write me book then?' asked Maureen.

'We'll have to lay hands on some novels, somehow,' said Harry, 'to see how it's done.' He had read a lot of books, biographies, history, special pleading, but was unacquainted with fiction, apart from his own.

157

'Oh, I've got bags of books!' said Maureen, laughing. 'You wait till you have to carry them!'

Indeed it seemed to Harry, as they furtively transferred Maureen's belongings from her small room at the top of the Hall to the caravan or the back seat of the Rolls that cold and darkening December afternoon, that most of them consisted of books.

'Shall we pinch the telly?' asked Maureen, as they looked around the denuded room.

'It won't work on my current,' said Harry.

'All right, we won't then.'

'I'll have it,' said Albert, who had been helping them with the carry. 'That's a colour set, that is. I've only got black and white.' Albert lived in the gatehouse at the end of the drive, so they put Maureen's colour television set in the back of the Rolls.

'Are we fit?' asked Harry. Maureen thought hard. 'I can't think of anything,' she said. 'I'd like to have said goodbye to Len, but he's gone home.'

'I'll say goodbye for you,' Albert offered. He had accepted without question Harry's need to go. He didn't bother to try to understand the reason. He would himself hold on here until a threat appeared, or the tedium of it all overcame his sense of safety.

'In the back then, Albert,' said Harry. Maureen, wrapped in many layers of clothes which Harry knew she would gradually discard as the modern heater he had himself installed warmed the front compartment, was sitting demurely beside the driver's seat. Harry switched on the ignition and set the 'Cold Start' lever on the boss of the steering wheel. Then he went round to the front of the car to turn the engine over by hand. It had a starter motor, but he preferred to conserve the battery. The car usually started at the second pull, as now. He retrieved the long starting handle, slid it in below the driving seat, and took up his position behind the wheel. He engaged second gear—first was superfluous, even with the caravan on tow—

and the equippage slid almost silently out of the orchard.

Albert and the colour television set were put down at the gatehouse.

'You know where I am,' said Albert, 'for a while at least, if you run into any trouble. I dare say we'll run up against each other anyway.'

Harry thought this unlikely, Albert not being a travelling man, but stoutly agreed. 'Bound to,' he said, 'bound to. Glad you were here, Albert. Made it possible for a while.'

'What more can we ask?' said Albert, adopting a position he assumed would appeal to Harry. He hefted the television set up on to his chest. 'Happy Christmas, Saucebottle. Ta-ta, Mave, me old darling.'

Harry and Maureen made their low-keyed farewells. Harry slipped the car into gear, first gear this time for reasons of his own. They moved off slowly, out of the lodge gates and into the high-hedged lane. Maureen snuffled briefly into a handkerchief. Then she noticed that Harry had opened the driver's door. 'What you doing?' she cried, alarmed.

'I like to stretch my legs,' said Harry. He stepped out on to the running board, then down to the ground, and closed the door. Walking beside the car, he reached in through the open window, moved the 'Cold Start' lever to zero and marginally adjusted the manual throttle on the steering boss. Then, with one hand resting gently on the steering wheel, he ambled along contentedly beside the huge, slowly purring limousine. The stubby gear lever, which needed no clutch to release it into neutral, and the long handle of the handbrake were within easy reach to the right of the steering wheel should he need to bring the equippage to a halt. Harry had proceeded like this, at various times, all over England and Wales.

Maureen said, 'What's going on? What are you doing out there?'

'Stretching my legs. I told you.'

'Are you going to do this for long, Harry? Aren't we ever going to go any faster?'

'Why go faster?' asked Harry. 'We aren't going anywhere.'

Maureen looked at him. Crazy man. But not an eejit. She accepted his right to be like that. She opened the fat, narrow-ruled exercise book on her lap and started to read her novel. It was rubbish, she decided. What she needed was personal experience. She glanced through the open window at Harry, happily walking beside the car. She shivered. Oh well.